TENERIFFE

CORPORAL OF THE GUARD

JASON ARNOLD BECKER

TENERIFFE
CORPORAL OF THE GUARD

iUniverse books may be ordered through booksellers or by contacting:

iUniverse
1663 Liberty Drive
Bloomington, IN 47403
www.iuniverse.com
1-800-Authors (1-800-288-4677)

Because of the dynamic nature of the Internet, any web addresses or links contained in this book may have changed since publication and may no longer be valid. The views expressed in this work are solely those of the author and do not necessarily reflect the views of the publisher, and the publisher hereby disclaims any responsibility for them.

Any people depicted in stock imagery provided by Thinkstock are models, and such images are being used for illustrative purposes only. Certain stock imagery © Thinkstock.

ISBN: 978-1-4917-8353-5 (sc)
ISBN: 978-1-4917-8352-8 (e)

Library of Congress Control Number: 2015921483

Print information available on the last page.

iUniverse rev. date: 2/26/2016

For the veterans of the wars in Iraq and Afghanistan
For my mother and father
For my immortal beloved, ED

1

"ARE YOU GAY, PRIVATE GAY? I'm asking *you* a question, Recruit! Hello! Hello, dumb ass! Are you gay, Private Gay? This requires a response from you, numb nuts! Hello! I can't hear you! You're not answering my question! Are you gay, Private Gay?" the brass lieutenant trumpets into Gay's ear, standing inches from the recruit's head and shouting into it as if it were a megaphone. "I can't hear you! You're gay! Aren't you, Gay? Well, aren't you? Private Gay! I mean really gaaaaay! Private Gaaaaaay!"

"No, no, sir," stutters Private Gay, standing at attention, watery eyed, staring straight ahead, body rigid in front of two marine officers.

"You aren't gay?" screams the lieutenant, feigning confusion. "It says right here that you're gay, Gay! This is Gay, right, Captain?"

The captain nods.

"How can you sit here and say that you're not gay, Gay?"

Private Gay is being interviewed in the Hotel Company commander's office of the Third Battalion recruit training depot at Parris Island, South Carolina. Parris Island is one of only two places in the country where enlisted marines are first indoctrinated into Marine Corps warrior training; the other recruit depot is located on the other side of the country in San Diego, California. Situated in this cramped, oddly shaped office approximately fifteen feet from the doorway is a gray and silver desk, behind which sits the captain. The space is almost three times as long as it is deep, and it is crowded with other desks and gray filing cabinets. Behind the captain's desk along the entire back wall of the room is a big green metal filing cabinet that comes up to about waist height. Above the enormous olive-drab cabinet are banks of clouded green glass windows. The windows appear to have been manufactured from recycled Coke bottles.

The occupants of the rectangular room are the blond-headed Captain Jones, reclining in his chair behind his desk; Lieutenant Wolf, who at first was sitting on the captain's desk with one foot on the ground and arms crossed; Private Gay, standing at attention a few feet in front of the captain's desk, facing the captain, eyes straight ahead, heels together, arms by his sides, hands in fists with his thumbs along the seams of his camouflaged trousers, shaking somewhat from his black boots to his bald head; and a cleaning party of five green recruits who just arrived a few days earlier to the Hotel Company to begin their recruit training and who are now turned to cleaning the company commander's office. The cleaning detail has paper towels, and they are using squirt bottles of Simple Green to wipe down everything in the office. One recruit has already emptied all the trash from the trash bins into one large bag and double-timed it to the green Dumpster in the cement courtyard. The other green recruits are cleaning at various positions around the office's crowded space while trying to be as inconspicuous as possible.

"You're sure that you're not gay, Private Gay?" the lieutenant sings again. "I freakin' know you're freakin' gay for a freakin' fact, Gay! It says right here! You're freakin' gay, Gay!" The lieutenant jams his index finger at a brown folder with a black seal on the front. "You're gay, Private Gay!"

"My name is Gay, sir, yes, sir, but I'm not gay, sir," says Private Gay in a quivering falsetto.

The lieutenant, who has reestablished himself atop the captain's desk, quickly and violently jumps off the desk and screams at the side of Gay's head again. "Oh, freakin' bullshit! You're completely frickin' gay! I'm a hundred percent sure! I got my gaydar on, dick wad, and it says that you're a flamin' freakin' faggot! And my gaydar is never wrong, never freakin' wrong! You're gay as freakin' hell, aren't you, Gay? You better tell us the freakin' truth, now, Gay. I mean it, Gay!"

"Yeah, Gay, you'd better tell us the truth for real, or there is no way we can help you," the captain calmly says. "See, if you tell us the truth about you being gay, well, we can probably get you out of here fast, quick, and in a hurry. But if you insist on this hardship crap about my momma's sick, and my daddy needs an operation, and my sister has a clubfoot, well, it's gonna take a while for the paperwork and stuff to go through. See what I mean, Private Gay? And I'm talkin' weeks and weeks of bullshit paperwork, maybe even months. But if you say that you are, in fact, gay, well hell, that's another story entirely. We can get you to a special separation company today where you won't have to be involved in any more training, and you'll only be there for less than two weeks, I think. Well, depends on the cycle, really, but three weeks at the latest, but maybe only a week and a half."

"Come on, Gay—just admit it," says Lieutenant Wolf. "You're gay as hell, right? That's all you gotta say. Just tell the truth. You can't control yourself. You love going to the showers and latherin' up with all the boys and bunking right next to all the guys in their skivvies, and it's just freakin' turnin' you on and makin' you crazy," says the lieutenant with his tongue out to the side and swirling his finger around the side of his head with a smile. But then Lieutenant Wolf gets deadly serious again in an instant and says through clenched teeth, "Right, Gay?"

"No, no, sir," says Gay, who is obviously painfully aware of the other recruits in the office.

"Oh, freakin' bullshit!" blasts the lieutenant. "You're so gay I can smell it coming out of your pores. You're gay for all the hot young studs that come here, and you can't control yourself, and you're worried that you might do something drastic to yourself or to the other young recruits here just mindin' their own business."

The lieutenant scans the small office space. Oddly, the cleaning party recruits are not paying attention to the scene and are still cleaning diligently.

"Come on, Gay! Just admit it now! You could be out yesterday. I'm kidding, but it would be fast! That way the captain can transfer you out immediately to some gay holding platoon with pink drapes on the windows and quilts on the racks—where you won't be a danger to the other recruits and you can be home in a week or so, just in time to enroll in ceramics class with all your bitchy little boyfriends."

There are some laughs from around the room, and Lieutenant Wolf has a big smile, showing his perfect white teeth. Lieutenant Wolf has a muscular, athletic build, as does Captain Jones. However, unlike the blond Captain Jones, whose hair is swept over to one side with a part, Lieutenant Wolf is darker skinned and sports a jet-black, high-and-tight flattop.

"You want to go home, right, Gay?" asks the captain.

Gay nods.

"You say you have to go home right now! You say it is absolutely imperative you get home right now and that you would do *anything* to leave, right, Gay? Well, boy, I'm giving you this, Gay! I'm gift wrapping it, Gay! The very best way and very only way is to just admit that you are really and truly gay, Gay, and then we can get this ball a-rolling! So look at me for a second, Gay, and carefully think about your answer, and think about what it is I'm asking you, Gay. Are you gay, Private Gay?"

"Yes," says Private Gay, looking down bashfully at his boots.

"Yes what, dip wad!" shouts Lieutenant Wolf.

"Yes, I am gay, sir!" says Gay, defeated yet hopeful.

"Oh my God! Captain! Oh my Gawd!" laughs Lieutenant Wolf. "I knew you were freakin' gay, Gay! You make me freakin' sick! I can't even stand to look at you! You little monkey freakin' fairy!"

"You're in deep shit, Private Gay," says the captain. "You know you just admitted to a federal offense, don't you?"

Private Gay's eyes grow large, and his mouth drops wide open in bewilderment.

"That's right, douche bag!" blasts Lieutenant Wolf. "A federal freakin' offense! We could send you to Leavenworth if we wanted to, you freakin' puke! You just admitted it to us and these other recruits right here."

The captain and the lieutenant look around the company office at the cleaning party, who again are apparently not paying any attention to the plight of poor Private Gay.

"Before you ever got here, you signed sworn affidavits that said you were *not* gay," the captain continues. "And now you're saying you lied—that your word means nothing! That's a criminal offense, jack-off! Do you remember all the paperwork, the tons of paperwork and oaths and signatures and initialing that you did, swearing to tell the truth back in your cushy little home way before you ever even got on the freakin' bus? Well, dipshit, that meant something! It may not have meant shit to you, dirtbag, but it meant something to the freakin' Marine Corps and the freakin' United States, and it feakin' meant something to us men of honor, dick!" The captain slams his fist into the metal desk. "What are we going to do with you, Gay? Jeez!" he hisses through clenched teeth.

"Now look, numb nuts, you've made the captain angry. I'm angry too, damn it! Good freakin' job, Marine. You have already managed to completely piss off two officers in the United States Marine Corps, and you're here already for what, like two weeks? I knew you were trouble from the get-go! Agh!" yells Lieutenant Wolf.

The room becomes quiet except for the sound of the cleaning party working diligently, and the lieutenant grows contemplative. "I mean, you're really freakin' gay, Gay? You're really freakin' gay?" says the lieutenant, sitting back down on the top of the desk, repeating himself, shaking his head pensively. "Maybe you're just a little gay, Gay? Maybe you like to do it with both boys *and* girls? 'Cause I just can't see it. Right, Captain? I mean I don't get it; I just can't understand. A woman's body is like a work of art. Like freakin' Italian art painted by Renaissance painters. Women have those full, pouty lips. Their skin is like silk. Their hair is so full and shiny and bouncy. Women are freakin' amazing, ugh. They're so soft, ugh, and freakin' warm. They're so freakin' cute! Right, Captain? And oh my God, the way they smell— ugh! The way they smell—ugh! Oh, for heaven's sake, the way a woman smells! I could almost lose my mind just thinking of the way a woman smells!"

"That's right, LT," says the captain in full agreement.

"And that hot LZ between their legs. Oh my Gawd! Okay, like just last night—just last night, Captain—I was smokin' the ass on this little fox I met at the O club."

"Oh, wait ... which one was that?" asks the captain.

"You remember that little petite one with the plaid miniskirt and the ponytail with the red ribbon?"

"Oh my gosh, no!" chortles the captain as he scoots his chair up closer to the desk and leans forward. "She was smokin' hot. She was tiny, but she had great big tits, right?" The captain holds his hands out in front of his chest, simulating a pair of oversize breasts.

"Yeah," laughs the lieutenant. "I'm smokin' her little ass, right, from behind, and these huge melons are flippin' and floppin' all over the place ..."

See, this is all wrong. We should start from the top and work our way down. So that way, we only clean once. And these paper towels are getting fouled way too quickly, and we're using way too many. When was the last time a cleaning party was even on this detail, anyway? Look at that hanging light in the center of the room; there must be an inch of dust on it. We have to hit that light before we go. It would make it three times brighter in here. Then we could see what we're doing better, and we could be more efficient. The captain could get a lot more work done, and the whole company would benefit. Methinks we could use some old rags that are maybe donated and buckets of clean water. This is a terrible waste of government funds.

"Oh, and the look on her face, Captain. It's all flush, and her little brow is scrunched up, and she's about to cry like Gay here, and she's saying the filthiest shit, like, 'Oh God, oh God, your cock is so hard!'" mimics the lieutenant in a high-pitched female voice.

I could get that green chair over there and bring it over here, and then I could use it to step up on top of this tall gray filing cabinet. Wasn't there a wooden stepladder out in the cement courtyard? Yeah, of course, a perfectly good ladder, just doing nothing but sitting out in the courtyard. That way I could get really high; that would make this job so much easier. But at least if I could get on the cabinet with the chair, then I could reach the top of the wall and maybe do the ceiling before we go.

"Captain, she wants to introduce me to one of her friends so we can do it at the same time. I mean I can't wait to have both of these chicks suckin' my dick together," crows the lieutenant. "Well, then she starts screaming, 'Harder, baby, harder, baby, spank my ass, daddy!'"

Jesus, do they use Simple Green to clean everything?

One of the recruits on the cleaning party makes a quick inhalation of air through his nostrils, creating a sound that attracts the attention of the captain and the lieutenant. The sniff is either an irritation from the chemical disinfectant's smell, a display of contempt, or the suppression of tears from an overwrought young man's heart miles and months away from any female on earth. The sniff may be a combination of all three sentiments, but it is more than likely that it is principally the latter of the three.

Lieutenant Wolf and Captain Jones's attention knifes to a big recruit in one of the far corners. The two officers see a recruit whose eyes are cast toward the ceiling and who is scrubbing as high on the wall as he can reach, standing on the tiptoes of his new black leather combat boots. The recruit is stocky and muscular like a linebacker. He is five feet and eleven inches tall with dark tanned skin and blue eyes.

"You recruits about finished?" asks the captain, clearing his throat.

"Detail, uh-ten-shun!" commands the big recruit. Four other camouflaged recruits snap to attention at various places in the room. "Sir, yes, sir!" shouts the big one.

"What's your name, Recruit?" asks the captain.

"Sir, Private Teneriffe, sir!"

"What do you think, Teneriffe?"

"Sir, this recruit thinks the lieutenant is full of crap, sir!"

The captain laughs. "No, what do you think about Gay here? Do you think he's gay?"

Teneriffe looks at the completely miserable Private Gay and says flatly, "He looks awright to me, sir."

"Very well," laughs the captain. "You recruits set your cleaning supplies down on the desks and report back to your platoon."

"Dismissed, aye, sir! Detail, fall out into the passageway!"

Teneriffe and the other recruits quickly set down their cleaning supplies and spill out into the passageway, but only after Teneriffe takes one last disparaging look at the central hanging light fixture.

Once all the recruits have lined up in a row, Teneriffe commands, "Detail, attention! Left face. Forward march!"

After marching a little way along the passageway, Teneriffe hears an older recruit whisper, "Ten, did you see that serious misappropriation of government funding?"

"Tell me about it, Cookie," says Teneriffe.

"Tee hee tee hee hee," laughs Cookie Jarvis. Cookie has a strange laugh that is low and quiet, just barely loud enough for Teneriffe to hear. It sounds like he is trying hard to suppress his mirth, but he is quite unable to prevent the sound from bubbling up to the surface.

MANY HOURS LATER, BACK IN the squad bay, it is getting close to lights-out for the platoon of fifty-three green recruits. The darkness on the other side of the barrack's clouded glass is ominous like the constant surf advancing and receding on a foamy, dark, desolate beach. The squad bay is a long, rectangular space. Gray metal racks double stacked into bunk beds take up most of the bay. Each set of racks has a green plywood footlocker on either end. The gray racks line both sides of the long room, with the ends a few feet away from the banks of clouded green windows that run the entire length of the space. About six feet from the racks toward the center of the room are two long yellow stripes painted on the floor. They run the entire length of the squad bay on both sides but end before the quarterdeck. At one end of the squad bay, the racks go almost all the way to the bulkhead, where there is a door to a concrete stairwell outside. This is the portal that the platoon uses whenever it goes outside or comes back inside en masse.

The platoon's squad bay is the third floor of a four-story redbrick building. *It seems a bit unfortunate to draw the third story, yet the fourth story would be worse,* thinks Teneriffe. The building is pleasing esthetically, not like the white Quonset huts in the dirt in *Gomer Pyle* but modern and austere quarters with plush green grass and live oaks and Spanish moss.

The big end of the squad bay narrows to a smaller passageway just past the quarterdeck with the drill instructors' office on the starboard side and the head on the port. The drill instructors' office has a large, rectangular window that looks out on to the quarterdeck but is always covered with a green curtain. The head on the left is furnished with about twenty white toilets with ebony seats in a long row with no partitions. Behind the toilets and separated by a bulkhead, there are showerheads along a wall in a square room. In another section of the head, a bulkhead separates white porcelain sinks and silver-trimmed mirrors from a white washer and dryer. Just beyond the second portal exiting the head, the passageway that separates the head and the drill instructors' office opens into a foyer whose only feature is a door on the port side that leads to an interior ladder well.

The platoon of recruits is gathered on the quarterdeck sitting Indian style, listening to the senior drill instructor, Gunnery Sergeant Morehouse, share his knowledge with his new recruits. At his sides are the gunny's assistant drill instructors, Staff Sergeant Carpenter and Sergeant Roebuck.

"And when it's mail call, clap the envelope between your hands," sneers Senior Drill Instructor Gunnery

Sergeant Morehouse, "like this." The gunnery sergeant makes a clapping motion, with one hand coming down vertically on the other. "I don't want any of you freakin' little monkeys to even come close to freakin' touching me."

Gunnery Sergeant Morehouse is a dark green marine with black horn-rimmed glasses. The marines have a unique way of describing race among their ranks. Marines are neither black nor white. They are dark green or light green. Senior Drill Instructor Gunnery Sergeant Morehouse is a dark green marine. The creases in his uniform look like they could cut someone, and the rest of his uniform and bearing are impeccable—every shiny surface shines, and every button is right in place. Gunny Morehouse is *the* lean, mean, fighting machine. There is no fat on Gunnery Sergeant Morehouse's densely muscled frame.

"So that's all I have, except fire watches, don't freakin' fall asleep on post; the duty officer will have all our asses in a sling! Staff Sergeant Carpenter, do you have anything to add?" The gunnery sergeant looks over his right shoulder to the giant Staff Sergeant Carpenter.

"Yuns got ten minutes till lights-out, ladies, so I suggest you write your little sweethearts, who are probably in the backseat of Jodi's car fogging up the windows as we speak!" The Staff Sergeant smiles broadly at his joke, showing more teeth than should be inside a human head. Those teeth in that giant, flat head make him look like an alligator or a crocodile.

To fully comprehend the Parris Island experience, it is absolutely imperative to understand that everything the drill instructors say is a holler, a scream, or a shout.

But even those words fall short of describing the strange cadences and melodies the drill instructors conjure. They stretch words, they sing words, they emphasize every other word at times. Sometimes the drill instructors lower their voices and speak in robotic tones. So when Staff Sergeant Carpenter says, "fogging up the windows as we speak," he stretches the word *speak* for several seconds, causing the sound to bounce off the walls and the inside of the recruits' skulls.

"Or even better yet," Sergeant Roebuck adds, "yous should work in groups on your drill or read your green monsters on some of the knowledge we covered today in class!" The green monster is the book that all marine recruits are issued at the beginning of training and is officially entitled *US Marine Guidebook of Essential Subjects.* "Remember, ladies, you will be tested!"

"That's right. That's good advice; that's right, ladies," agrees Staff Sergeant Carpenter. "And if you need to speak with the senior drill instructor because yuns are having some feminine hygiene problems! Yuns will be allowed to come see him in the drill instructors' office tonight! Before lights-out! Yuns have got ten minutes! Turn to!"

"So hold it the freak down!" thunders Drill Instructor Sergeant Roebuck.

Another oddity about the way the drill instructors speak is that they never say the *f* word. In place of saying *fuck* or *motherfucker,* the marines say *freak, freakin',* or *mother freaker.* It is plainly clear almost immediately after arriving at basic training that someone high up has ordered the marines at Parris Island not to use the *f* word. However, because the marines use *freak* or *freakin'* in such a universal fashion all the time, in all their speech, it is difficult not to envision the very word that they are avoiding.

The drill instructors turn and are about to walk back to their office when Sergeant Roebuck whispers into Staff Sergeant Carpenter's ear. The staff sergeant has to bend his neck down and to the side to hear him.

Drill Instructor Staff Sergeant Carpenter straightens to his full towering height, does a complete about-face, and looks directly at Teneriffe. The staff sergeant, bearing a big, toothy, gnarled alligator smile, booms, "Oh yeah! And Teneriffe! The senior drill Instructor needs to see you in his office before lights out!"

The drill instructors quickly turn and, in a flash, are gone back into their office.

Huh! What did he say? I need to see the who in the what? No way! I thought I'd have at least a few minutes to read a spell. Calm down. Calm down. It could be good news. Calm the freak down! Perhaps if I get in line quickly, I can get back in time to read for maybe five minutes or so ... No way! This is bull! Why do I have to see the drill instructors? I don't want to see the drill instructors!

This is the first time since their arrival at Parris Island that the recruits have been given the opportunity to enter the drill instructors' office to speak freely with the drill instructors. Teneriffe doesn't wait long. He takes just enough time to stow his green monster away in his green plywood footlocker, but somehow four other recruits have beaten him to the line that forms outside the drill instructors' office.

Now Teneriffe waits patiently outside the office against the bulkhead behind the recruits in front of him.

On the bulkhead next to the open entranceway is a red, square plywood plaque. On the center of this red plaque is the outline of a yellow handprint. Stenciled yellow letters under the handprint read, "Knock five times. Ask permission to enter."

The color of the yellow handprint and the general nature of the sign remind Teneriffe of the yellow boot prints that the recruits stand on the first thing after getting off the busses at Parris Island. There are yellow boot prints literally all over the place at Parris Island. They sit in columned rectangles in front of most buildings to show the platoons of raw green recruits how to assemble as a unit. On the spring night when Teneriffe's platoon debarked the silver chartered Greyhound bus, the set of yellow boot prints on the street illuminated by the street lamps in front of the old receiving barracks was confusing. Teneriffe, who was one of the last recruits off the bus, having grown accustomed to sitting in the back of chartered busses on long road trips when he played for his school's football squad, positioned his feet correctly on his set of yellow boot prints, looked into the faces of his new platoon in the artificial light, and then turned around so that he was going in the wrong direction along with the rest of his platoon. He should have been in the back of the formation, but he was instead now in the position of the First Squad leader.

The receiving drill instructors were beside themselves with glee. Those marines had seen a lot during their time at Parris Island, but it truly had to be rare to see a whole platoon get on the boot prints going in the wrong direction.

"I can't believe what I'm seeing. Glory be! Do I see what I'm seein'? Oh my freakin' God! I can't believe my freakin' eyes!" laughed the head receiving drill instructor. "No! Quick, someone get a camera! I can't believe this shit! Are we the luckiest sons of bitches alive? Ha ha ha ha!"

Derisive laughter surrounded the platoon.

"You numb nuts have managed to screw up the simplest thing we have to do here at Parris Island. I guess we like to call it getting on the freakin' yellow boot prints going in the right freakin' direction! Ha ha ha ha ha! So! Well, good luck for the next three months with the rest of all that!" Then the receiving drill instructor took a long pause. "But! We are marines! And we, being United States Marines, are going to use this little miscarriage of natural human reason and dignity as a training opportunity! You all are going in the wrong direction! We want to make you go in the right direction! So we are going to teach you to do an about-face! Take your right toe and move it to the back of your left heel. Now your feet should look like seven o'clock if your feet were dials on a clock."

"Does he mean a.m. or p.m.?" whispered a recruit.

Several recruits shushed the confused recruit.

"Now go back on your right heel and turn around with your heels coming together into a V! Ready! Okay! About-face! No! No! No! Do it again! Try it again! About-face! Oh good heavens! Try it again! Do it again! About-face! Holy shit! No way! Do it again! Let's try it again! About-face!"

Teneriffe looks at the red sign outside the drill instructor's office. *No! No! No! Good heavens. We were doing it wrong then, and now the recruits are doing it wrong on this red board and yellow handprint. You've got to slap the shit out of it like we used to do on each other's football helmets. Ya got to smack it hard and fast with your open palm: one, two, three, four, five! Smack!*

The four recruits that went into the office in front of Teneriffe all lightly rapped on the yellow hand with their knuckles as if it were the door of a house back home. Teneriffe thinks he can do better.

"No! For the tenth time, you can't have special hardship leave for freakin' sake! Now get the freak out of my office, you maggot mother freaker!" Teneriffe hears Senior Drill Instructor Gunnery Sergeant Morehouse bellow. A recruit comes darting out the office portal as if propelled from a slingshot.

Okay! Here goes! Flap! *Good hit!*

Two! Flap! *Good play!*

Three! Flap! *Yeah, baby!*

Four! Flap! *Woohoo!*

Five! Flap! *Yeah, come on!*

"Sir, Private Teneriffe requests permission to enter the drill instructors' office, sir!"

"Come in, come in, let's go!" sneers Gunnery Sergeant Morehouse. The tone of his voice is almost pure barely restrained disgust. The gunnery sergeant sits behind his desk facing the passageway. To the gunnery sergeant's right stand his two assistant drill instructors, Staff Sergeant Carpenter and Sergeant Roebuck. Both the assistant drill instructors are light green marines. Staff Sergeant Carpenter stands closest to the desk, towering over the small room at about six six or six seven. He has a face that looks like it's been slammed with a frying pan in one of those *Looney Toons* cartoons. Staff Sergeant Carpenter is standing between the gunnery sergeant's green and silver desk and Drill Instructor Sergeant Roebuck, who stands about a foot shorter and facing perpendicular to the gunnery sergeant. Sergeant Roebuck has a permanent scowl and a curled upper lip that looks like it's been stitched that way.

Drill Instructor Sergeant Roebuck snarls, "*Private* Teneriffe—ha! You isn't even a freakin' recruit."

Huh? I'm not a recruit? Teneriffe strides to the center of the room in the middle of the three men and then turns to Staff Sergeant Carpenter at attention and says, "Sir, Recruit Teneriffe reporting as ordered, sir!"

"Wrong! Wrong! Wrong!" bellows Drill Instructor Staff Sergeant Carpenter. His head sways spastically from side to side when he says these words. He holds his head tilted to the left. "Wrong!" Then he throws his head all the way to the right. "Wrong!" Then he throws his head all the way to the left. "Wrong! Ya know what? No! Get the freak out and try it again! Get the freak out!"

"And get that dumb-shit look off your face!" adds Sergeant Roebuck.

Teneriffe strides back out into the hallway, and he faces the red sign on the bulkhead with the stenciled yellow letters.

Huh. Something was wrong? What's wrong? Oh, I wasn't specific enough. I was too succinct; I'm not reporting as ordered. Ha, reporting as ordered. That was stupid—probably too much TV. I should have asked permission to speak. I'll ask permission to speak. Still, I thought I would have at least five minutes to read a bit! Teneriffe sees the yellow palm print and reads the message, "Knock five times. Ask permission to enter." *Maybe not ten minutes to read and relax but at least …*

Five! Bam! Teneriffe slams his palm into the wood, which seems to rattle the concrete bulkheads. *I've got to become a better speaker!*

Four! Bam! Now, Teneriffe's left hand is on the cold masonry wall too for better force and balance. *Hey! This feels good!*

Three! Bam! Teneriffe is going way back now. *Summer camp and two-a-days!*

Two! Bam! *Friday night lights, cheerleaders, and marching bands*!

One! Bam! "Sir, Recruit Teneriffe requests permission to enter the drill instructors' office, sir!"

"Come in, Teneriffe," says the Senior Drill Instructor Gunnery Sergeant Morehouse. There is something new in his tone that Teneriffe can't decipher. All three drill instructors are there still.

Drill Instructor Sergeant Roebuck sneers, "What is it now, Tene-*grief?* You got a boo-boo ah?"

Still standing equidistant from all three men and facing Drill Instructor Staff Sergeant Carpenter, Teneriffe shouts, "Sir, Recruit Teneriffe requests permission to speak with—"

Staff Sergeant Carpenter interrupts with his head swaying from side to side twice as fast now, "Wrong, wrong, wrong! No! Hell no! Ya know what? Sonofabitch! I can't believe this shit! Get the freak out of the *gunny's* office and try it again!" Now the peculiar tone has entered his voice as well.

Sergeant Roebuck adds, "Get the freak out!"

Before Teneriffe can reach the passageway, Senior Drill Instructor Gunnery Sergeant Morehouse commands, "First, turn the freakin' lights out, Tenegrief. They've gotten way too much free time already!" Gunnery Sergeant Morehouse sneers this last order at Teneriffe like it's all his fault.

What the ... what the ... what the freak?

Teneriffe strides through the portal and onto the quarterdeck. All the recruits in the platoon are sitting on their footlockers looking down at their green monsters, and they all look up in unison at Teneriffe standing on the center of the quarterdeck. More than a few have concerned looks on their faces. Teneriffe tries to hide a smile.

No other recruit has turned out the lights before. I got to make this good. Teneriffe trumpets out, "Ten seconds until lights out!"

There is an explosion of activity as the recruits stow away and secure their belongings in their green plywood footlockers. Immediately the recruits also begin to chant in unison, counting down from ten. "Ten, nine, eight, seven, six, five, four, three, two, one, discipline, sir, discipline, d-i-s-c-i-p-l-i-n-e, discipline, sir, discipline!"

Each recruit jumps into his rack at attention. As the recruits land on their racks, their voices echo off the vaulted cement ceiling. Discipline rings all around them. Teneriffe flips the bank of large, black switches that open the circuits, extinguishing the lights. In the semidarkness betrayed only by the red lights that mark the exits and the white light from the drill instructors' office, discipline can be heard faintly resounding through the walls from another platoon either above or below. All the marines lie still at attention in their racks.

"Fire watch, post!" commands Teneriffe. Two camouflaged recruits step out from between the racks and begin to walk slowly in opposite directions up and down the long, dark squad bay. "Tonight, Marines! Rest and dream of glory in battle! Sacrifice your worthless, punk ass lives to those who have paid the ultimate price in defense of our great country! And good Lord, founder and creator of the United States Marine Corps, please look after those that will go hungry tonight! Oo rah!"

"Oo rah!" Responds the whole platoon in unison, lying on their racks at attention.

"At ease!" commands Teneriffe. The exhausted recruits relax in their racks. There is an audible exhalation by fifty-plus young men and then a few laughs and then quiet.

The pride and esprit de corps that Teneriffe feels fade quickly when confronted with the impossible task of finding out why he is being summoned to the drill instructors' office in the first place. It seems to him at this moment that he will never get to sleep ever again.

I'm doing something wrong! I'm doing something wrong!

Teneriffe turns from the platoon of recruits lying in their racks. He paces back the ten or so steps to the open doorway of the drill instructors' office, and he again looks at the red plywood sign with the yellow handprint. Teneriffe reads its directive once more and feels his face grow red with anger and frustration at his inability to understand what he is doing wrong in front of the three drill instructors.

I ain't doin' nothin' wrong! Maybe I'm not knocking hard enough. That's it! Everything else is just perfect, but the DIs, God bless their old souls, are having trouble hearing me knock!

Five! Woppha! Ten hits the wooden plaque with rage. *Why am I always surrounded by all these dudes!*

Four! Woppha! *I ain't doin' nothin' wrong!*

Three! Woppha! *They're laughing at me—that's the funny tone in their voices.*

Two! Woppha! *Yaaaaaaaah waaaaaaaaaay!*

One! Woppha! "Sir, Private Teneriffe requests permission to enter the drill instructors' office, sir!"

"Come in Tenegrief," sneers Senior Drill Instructor Gunnery Sergeant Morehouse.

"What now, Tenegrief? You want some freakin' milk and cookies too?" says Sergeant Roebuck.

"Sir, Recruit Teneriffe requests permission to speak with—"

"Look, Tenegrief, when you enter a freakin' room, you always address the highest ranking person in the room, okay, not the one that looks like your freakin' father. Besides, I'm your freakin' father now anyways. Now what the freak did you have to speak with me about?"

Oh right. Teneriffe turns slightly so that now he is squarely facing Gunnery Sergeant Morehouse behind his desk instead of Staff Sergeant Carpenter.

Okay, wait—what? What the freak do I have to speak about? What the freak do I have to speak about? What the freak?

"His *mother*," says Staff Sergeant Carpenter. Sergeant Roebuck snickers.

Teneriffe totally breaks bearing and cocks his head back over his right shoulder, as if by x-ray vision and super hearing he can see through the bulkhead whether any of the other recruits lying in their racks heard those last two words.

"Right, freak, your mother called the company office today, Tenegrief. That's right—yo momma called and spoke with the company commander, Captain Jones, today. Seems she hasn't heard from you in a while and is worried about you," says Gunnery Sergeant Morehouse with a big smile. This is a new look for the gunnery sergeant, and it's probably scarier than his scowl. His teeth are like huge marble tombstones protruding jaggedly at different angles in a graveyard.

"What's the matter, Tenegrief? Don't you love your mommy?" teases Sergeant Roebuck.

"Yeah, Tenegrief, why do you wanna hurt your mommy so?" Staff Sergeant Carpenter says with that peculiar tone.

"So look, check it out, if everybody's momma calls up the company office all the freakin' time, we're not gonna be able to get a lot of work and shit done, see," sneers Gunnery Sergeant Morehouse. "So write yo momma a freakin' letter once in a while or call her now and freakin' then, okay, Tenegrief? Now get the freak out of my office!"

"Dismissed, aye, sir!" Teneriffe about-faces and begins to stride out of the office, but just as he reaches the passageway, he hears Gunnery Sergeant Morehouse say, "And Tenegrief, you're the First Squad leader from now on."

Freakin' great!

FIRE WATCH IS NOT AN easy duty. You'd think that after working harder in a day in basic training than ever before in your life, at least you would have a good night of uninterrupted sleep. That is simply not the case at Parris Island. Most every night, each recruit wakes from a dead sleep to walk for an hour on fire watch before waking another exhausted recruit to get up and get dressed and walk the dark squad bay for another hour. Sometimes, the exhausted recruit simply lies down in his rack and goes back to sleep.

Marching countless times toward either stairwell, Teneriffe looks into that dark void on the other side of the porthole and tries to conjure an apparition looking back from the other side. At the main stairwell window, Teneriffe always finds comfort in the slow, steady breathing of the sleeping rows of marines in the racks nearby. The other porthole to the interior stairwell is different. A heavy, golden pine–varnished wooden door inset with a large, rectangular glass wire window opens into an antechamber, an empty cubical space separated from the quarterdeck by a passageway. The antechamber at night has sort of its own strange, ethereal green glow. Perhaps it is the light bouncing off the light-green glazed bulkheads.

Teneriffe is at that interior porthole starring into the dark glass door, trying to look beyond the dim reflection of his own image to something deeper, something unseeable, perhaps something unknowable. Suddenly, with a swoosh of green darkness and smoke, the door swings open, and in strides a green-camouflaged Lieutenant Wolf. The lieutenant is covered, and the creases on his utility uniform are starched and pressed. He wears a green duty war belt and a firearm. The fire watch is unarmed at this early stage of basic training, but they are still covered and are wearing war belts.

Teneriffe, sharply at attention, with a salute but in a whisper, says, "Attention on deck!" Cookie Jarvis, at the small end of the squad bay, snaps to attention. Lieutenant Wolf strides quickly to face Teneriffe and cuts a quick salute. Teneriffe cuts his hand from the bill of his cover to the right seam of his camouflaged trouser.

"Nothing to report at this time, sir; all is quiet!" says Teneriffe quietly but alertly.

"Good," says Lieutenant Wolf. "What is your first general order?"

"Sir, this private's first general order is to take charge of this post and all government property in view, sir!"

"What is your second general order?" demands Lieutenant Wolf.

"Sir, this private's second general order is to walk my post in a military manner, keeping always on the alert and observing everything that takes place within sight or hearing, sir!"

"What is your third general order?"

"Sir, this private's third general order is to report all violations of orders I am instructed to enforce, sir!"

"What are the signs of heat exhaustion?"

"Sir, the signs of heat exhaustion are headache, excessive sweating, dizziness, muscle cramps, and clammy skin, sir."

"What are the symptoms of heatstroke?"

"Sir, the symptoms of heatstroke are lack of sweating, hot dry skin, headache, rapid pulse, dizziness, mental confusion, and collapse, sir," says Teneriffe, eyes straight ahead like laser beams.

"Which is the more serious of the two heat conditions?" asks Lieutenant Wolf.

"Sir, the more serious of the two heat conditions is heatstroke, because the marine may already be unconscious and needs to be submerged under cold water, if available, sir, as soon as possible, sir!"

"What year was the Declaration of Independence signed?"

"Sir, the Declaration of Independence was signed in 1776, sir," says Teneriffe.

"When was the Marine Corps founded?"

"Sir, the Marine Corps was founded on November 10, 1775, sir."

"What is the Marine Corps's insignia?"

"Sir, the Marine Corps's insignia is an eagle, globe, and anchor, sir."

"What do the eagle, globe, and anchor represent?"

"Sir, the eagle stands for the Marine Corps's service to our nation, the globe represents our long and glorious history throughout the world, and the anchor signifies the marines' storied naval traditions, sir."

"What makes up the physical fitness test?"

"Sir, the physical fitness test consists of sit-ups, pull-ups, and a three-mile run, sir."

"How often do marines take the physical fitness test?"

"Sir, marines take the physical fitness test at least twice a year, sir."

"What is the max number of sit-ups on the test?"

"Sir, the max number of sit-ups is eighty, sir."

"What is the max number of pull-ups on the test?"

"Sir, the max number of pull-ups is twenty, sir."

"What score represents a perfect score on the physical fitness test?"

"Sir, three hundred is a perfect score on the physical fitness test."

"What was your score on today's practice physical fitness test, Private?"

"Sir, this marine scored a two ninety-two, sir."

"What were your numbers, Private?"

"Sir, this marine did twenty pull-ups, eighty sit-ups, and did the run in nineteen minutes and twenty seconds, sir."

"You need to work on that run, don't you, Private?"

"Sir, yes, sir."

"What does NBC stand for?"

"Sir, NBC is nuclear, biological, and chemical, sir."

"How long do you have to don your gas mask once the alarm has been sounded?"

"Sir, the time allowed to don the gas mask after the alarm has been sounded is nine seconds, sir."

"What are some of the indicators of a biological or chemical attack?"

"Sir, the signs of a biological or chemical attack are suspicious liquids on the ground or on plants, unexplained smoke or mist, dead animals, and suspicious odors, sir."

"Um, okay," says Lieutenant Wolf, clearly trying to think of another question.

Teneriffe sees the lieutenant look up and to the left.

Wow, really? 'Cause I can go all day … well, night.

"Who wears a silver oak leaf on their collar?"

Oh, that's an easy one. My dad! "Sir, a lieutenant colonel wears a silver oak leaf, sir."

The other fire watch on duty, Cookie Jarvis, forgotten in the darkness and far enough down the passageway to go unnoticed but close enough to hear the challenges, makes the unmistakable sound of a contemptuous sniff.

Lieutenant Wolf's head snaps in the direction of the sound.

"As you were," says Lieutenant Wolf. Now the lieutenant is looking back into Teneriffe's face. "As you were. Carry on, fire watch!"

"Carry on, aye, sir," says Teneriffe as he cuts a sharp salute.

Lieutenant Wolf returns the courtesy and is gone back through the darkening portal.

Cookie Jarvis saunters up behind Teneriffe, who is peering into the porthole's dark, smoky glass after the lieutenant.

"What you looking at, Tenerooski?" laughs Cookie Jarvis, and he smacks the back of Teneriffe's bald head. "Tee hee tee hee hee. You look like you got some bad intentions there, Marine. How long was he gonna question you for?"

"For real," says Teneriffe. "I didn't miss anything either."

"Guess you shouldn't have called him full of crap in the captain's office," says Cookie Jarvis. "That was awesome!"

"Hey, Cookie, what do you say if you don't know the answer to one of the questions?"

"You say that you don't know the answer at this time but that you will find out the correct answer as soon as possible, sir. Thank you, sir!"

"Why do you add, 'Thank you, sir'?"

"They're gentlemen. It can't hurt you to be polite," says Cookie. "Sit down, Ten. I have a surprise." The two recruits sit down against the bulkhead. The tiled blocks are cool against their backs on an otherwise stifling Southern spring night.

"You'd think it would be enough just to be up and walking my post at freakin' the middle of the night," says Teneriffe.

"Yeah, he should give you a promotion," says Cookie Jarvis, tearing into a crisp brown paper and silver foil wrapper.

"Yeah, he should make me a DI. Hey, what ya got there, Cookie?" says Teneriffe, rubbing his hands together.

Cookie Jarvis pulls out a Hershey's chocolate bar and exclaims, "Time for some contraband! It is zero three forty-five, by the way." Cookie Jarvis breaks the chocolate bar and gives half to Teneriffe. "Here, you're gonna need this," says Cookie Jarvis.

"God, it will be reveille soon. Good googly moogly." Teneriffe takes a bite of his chocolate rectangles. "Oh, wow! This is the best thing I've ever had in my entire life. Oh my God. When was the last time we've eaten anything this good? I'll tell you when—never!"

"It has to be months and months ago," says Cookie. "So how are you holding up with all the fun and games?"

"Super. I love the beach. I hope we get to go again today," says Teneriffe.

The beach is a term that the drill instructors use for one particularly grueling activity on the training schedule. The instructors call it the beach because it is a large rectangular pit filled with sand on the side of one of the barracks. The platoon marches into the sandpit, and then the drill instructors make the platoon do exercises like sit-ups, bend-and-reaches, mountain climbers, push-ups, jumping jacks, and so on. Only now, the sand sticks to the recruits' sweaty bodies and gets all in their camouflage uniforms.

"Yeah, right," laughs Cookie Jarvis. "Not exactly like I pictured it. Where were the bikinis?"

"Yeah, no water either," says Teneriffe.

"Yeah, no waves," whispers Cookie Jarvis.

"Yeah, no fishes!" Sugar and caffeine are starting to tap Teneriffe's heart.

"No boats either," laughs Cookie Jarvis, motioning with his hands for Teneriffe to keep it down.

"No volleyball," says Teneriffe, whispering again.

"No surfers."

"No reclining chairs."

"No big giant umbrellas."

"No buds."

The two recruits settle down, sitting quietly for a few moments, enjoying the magical confection before them. Teneriffe sits starring at the shiny deck, thinking how to endure these last few minutes on fire watch before he is allowed to return to his rack to catch up on some much-needed sleep. Then a thought comes to Teneriffe's sleepy mind. It has been annoying him since arriving at Parris Island.

"Hey, Cookie, why do the DIs pick on Hay Fly the way they do? Hay Fly! It doesn't seem right to me."

Hay Fly is the nickname the drill instructors have given to Private Helfe for no particular reason except that the drill instructors love to bastardize everyone's names. In this particular case, it appears a rather fitting nickname for Private Helfe, who is skinny and not very substantial. He is pasty white and has only one speed—slow. He seems to have difficulty performing even the simplest of tasks. The drill instructors always blame Hay Fly as an excuse to inflict punishment on the platoon, but it seems to Teneriffe, at least, that a lot of recruits are making the same mistakes as Hay Fly. Teneriffe feels Hay Fly is being unfairly singled out for the blame, and he believes that

Hay Fly is an all right guy that maybe just needs a little encouragement.

"I don't know," says Cookie Jarvis, also gazing at the shiny deck. "I do not know the answer to that question at this time, but I will find out as soon as possible, sir. Thank you, sir."

Both marines chuckle a bit and then sit silently again for a spell chewing on the pride of Hershey, Pennsylvania.

"Well, you should wake up Private Bulloch, and we should walk our post again," says Cookie Jarvis.

"Why? Do you think Lieutenant Wolf will be back soon?" Teneriffe asks sarcastically.

"Yeah, probably," replies Cookie seriously. "Probably got some more of them fancy questions for ya, boy, like who killed the Kennedys? How do they get the caffeine out of the coffee beans in decaf coffee? Compare and contrast Jungian and Freudian psychology."

"How *do* they get the caffeine out of the coffee beans?" asks Teneriffe.

Cookie Jarvis stands up and straightens out his wrinkled utilities and reblouses his trousers by bending over and stretching tight his trouser legs using the green elastic bands (called boot bands) against the upper part of his boots. "Oh, and Ten," says Cookie Jarvis, "hurry and vanquish the recreant Green Knight so we can all get some sleep around here. Tee hee tee hee hee."

Huh? A question forms in Teneriffe's sleep-deprived mind, but as Cookie Jarvis is sidling away down the dark squad bay, he asks the more pertinent one. "Hey, Cookie, who's my relief?"

"Oh, yeah, you are. I traded it for the chocolate with Cubano."

"What? No way! Freakin' great. Thanks a lot," whispers Teneriffe. *No more sleep for the rest of the night. Today should be real fun!*

Cookie's one-of-a-kind laugh bubbles out and echoes off the cold bulkheads, fading slowly down the long, dark passageway. "Tee hee tee hee hee."

It's Sunday, and most of the recruits are sitting on their footlockers, reading and writing quietly. The far stairwell opens up, and a strange recruit from some other platoon steps out into the passageway. He tries to stride unnoticed to the drill instructors' office, but the guide, a Puerto Rican, six foot six and lean, shouts, "Strange private on deck!"

The platoon, in unison, roars like a jet engine, "Strange private on deck! Freeze, Private, freeze!" The echo slams off the green bulkheads. The strange recruit flinches from the boom and freezes in place.

The guide is a position given to one of the recruits in each platoon. It is a special position reserved for the top recruit who demonstrates excellent leadership potential. The guide carries the guidon stick with the red and gold flag that bears the platoon's number in front of the platoon whenever the platoon marches in formation, and he supervises the four squad leaders. It is a special distinction that many of the recruits hope to attain, but only a select few ever do.

The guide, who sits on the first foot locker just before the quarterdeck and some fifteen feet from the drill instructors' office, springs up and, in a moment, stands in front of the strange private, barring his way. Looking down, he says menacingly, "Whaddaya want?"

The strange private, at attention, says, "I have a note for your senior drill instructor, Gunnery Sergeant Morehouse, from the company office."

"Okay, follow me," says the guide. The guide stops in front of the drill instructors' office and slaps the yellow handprint five times. "The guide requests permission to enter the drill instructors' office, sir!"

"What is it, Guide?" yells Gunnery Sergeant Morehouse.

"Sir, strange private says he has a note from the captain, sir!"

"Okay, send 'im in and get the freak out of my sight, Guide!"

The guide gives the strange private one last menacing look down his nose with balled-up fists and flared lats.

Later that evening on the quarterdeck, the platoon is again gathered around for classroom, sitting Indian style in rows facing the DIs' office. "… and Hay Fly, if you freakin' touch me again during mail call, the next letter yo momma gets will be a freakin' condolence letter!" sneers Gunnery Sergeant Morehouse through bared teeth and curled lips.

"Tee hee tee hee hee."

"Okay," Gunnery Sergeant Morehouse says in a conversational tone. "Staff Sergeant Carpenter says most of you guys are coming around, so keep up the good work." Gunny Morehouse displays a big, crooked smile with those tombstone-white teeth surrounded by thick, black, tobacco-stained lips. "Okay, yuns got ten minutes till lights-out. And yuns still have plenty to think about with your drilling and your green monster, so hold it the freak down. And fire watches, truly, the duty officer is all over the place, so watch your freakin' asses. And don't even think of falling asleep on fire watch, or I'll beat the shit out of you myself, and I don't care what the freakin' mothers of America have to say." The gunnery sergeant looks at Teneriffe.

Jeez!

"Sergeant Roebuck, it's all yours!" Gunnery Sergeant Morehouse and Staff Sergeant Carpenter turn and stride confidently into the drill instructors' office.

"Aye, Senior Drill Instructor Gunnery Sergeant Morehouse, sir!" shouts Sergeant Roebuck. "Okay, you babies, write your sweethearts or your mommies!" Sergeant Roebuck looks at Teneriffe.

Oh, come on!

"Yous got thirty minutes till lights-out; if yous have a problem, speak to yuns squad leaders or to the guide! Turn to!" Sergeant Roebuck about-faces and then strides like a self-satisfied bulldog into the drill instructors' office.

Five minutes pass as the recruits quietly sit on their footlockers. Some recruits practice their drill maneuvers in small groups. The guide is at the far end of the squad bay with two recruits working on saluting.

Teneriffe, sitting on his footlocker reading his green monster, is approached by another recruit. "Hey, Ten, could you help me with some of this knowledge stuff? I ain't doing too good with the testing and shit, but you ain't missed nothin' I heard. 'Cause, I mean, I know a lot of this shit, but I just can't say it out loud, ya know?"

"Sure, of course," says Teneriffe, closing his green monster. "Well, what about your general orders? Do you know them, and can you explain what they mean?"

"See, yeah, that's what I'm talkin' about. See, Ten, I know them, but I can't really explain them, ya know what I mean, dude?"

"Well, try to think of the pictures in the book instead of the words. See, put yourself into that picture, dude," says Teneriffe. "Let's take the first one, 'to take charge of this post and all government property within view.'" Teneriffe opens the green monster to the page. "Think of that picture. You're there, dude. Try to see it in your mind."

"Yeah, dude, I get it."

"You're on that fence, bro."

"Yeah."

"You're strapped with your M16A2, locked and loaded, bro! You're on guard duty, you're on alert, and there's some bad mamma jammas all in the wire and shit. And what is the first thing you're gonna do, bro?"

"Yeah, bro! I'm gonna take charge of my post and all government property, dude!" says the other recruit excitedly.

"Hell yeah, you are, bro!" says Teneriffe.

Teneriffe and the other recruit continue to visualize the eleven general orders, only now they put themselves into the simple, funny pictures inside the green monster.

Suddenly, the stairwell door at the interior portal swings open, and a dark figure comes striding down the passageway toward the drill instructors' office. Teneriffe jumps up beside the other recruit. The other recruit begins to shout, "Strange private!" It is not a strange private but Captain Jones striding down the passageway. Misidentifying the captain for a strange private would be a grave mistake.

Teneriffe quickly gets behind the recruit, muzzling him with one hand over his wet and slimy mouth before shouting, "Attention on deck!"

Teneriffe gets elbowed in the ribs for his troubles, but the whole platoon snaps to attention. The squad bay, which only seconds earlier was awash in kinetic activity during free time and peer training, is now completely silent and still.

The captain stops before the drill instructors' office and looks at the platoon of green-camouflaged men all in line or in between the racks. "As you were, Recruits!"

The captain strides into the drill instructors' office. Gunnery Sergeant Morehouse sits behind his desk facing the entranceway. Staff Sergeant Carpenter and Sergeant Roebuck sit in green metal government chairs with small green pads on the arms and green-padded seats. The chairs are against the bulkhead to the left of Gunnery Sergeant Morehouse's desk facing the large, rectangular draped window that looks out onto the quarterdeck.

Gunnery Sergeant Morehouse says, "Attention on deck!"

The three men quickly rise to attention. Staff Sergeant Carpenter and Sergeant Roebuck are as straight as arrows, chins up, chests out. Gunnery Sergeant Morehouse's attention is different. He is at attention, but his arms and legs are bent at the joints as if they couldn't straighten out completely even if someone tried to pull on them. His chest is not out, either, but every muscle is taut and hard as steel.

Gunnery Sergeant Morehouse says, "Evenin', Captain. Two recruits on light duty. That's all, sir."

"Very good. At ease," says the captain. The three drill instructors snap to parade rest. "How's the drilling, Gunny? You gonna win the whole thing this time?"

Captain Jones is referring to the final drill competition between the four platoons of the series that occurs near the end of basic training. The drilling competition is the most sought-after victory for any platoon at basic warrior training, and close-order drill is a usual part of every day on the training schedule. To the marines, it is the true measure of how well a platoon can demonstrate teamwork and discipline. Gunny Morehouse has never won the close-order drill competition, and the company commander is needling him.

"I don't know, Captain. We got a bunch of chuckleheads this time around," says Gunnery Sergeant Morehouse. "You know these are the ones that got on the yellow boot prints backward." All the men laugh. "Let's just say I'll be happy if they throw the hand grenades in the right direction, sir. Anyways, I thought Gunny Mesceri was your boy."

Gunnery Sergeant Morehouse is referring to Senior Drill Instructor Gunnery Sergeant Mesceri, the head drill instructor for First Platoon on the ground floor of the barracks. Gunny Morehouse is suggesting that the whole competition may be rigged. It is Gunny Morehouse who is now needling the captain.

Changing the topic quickly, the captain laughs and says, "What do you make of this recruit, Teneriffe?"

Ever since the evaluation in the company office and Lieutenant Wolf's questioning of Teneriffe on fire watch, Teneriffe has been a recruit singled out as having leadership potential.

"Sir, he's a good man, Captain," Staff Sergeant Carpenter answers confidently, jutting out his rock-solid chin.

"Right, yes, he's a good man—a great man, Captain!" agrees Sergeant Roebuck.

"A great man?" says Staff Sergeant Carpenter incredulously with his face now contorted into a grimace and looking down at Sergeant Roebuck.

Sergeant Roebuck, realizing he is perhaps overstating his intention, says, "Well, all right, he's a good man, sir!"

Staff Sergeant Carpenter straightens back to normal and, facing to the front, says with an air of contentment, "He's a fine man, sir!"

Sergeant Roebuck says, "Right, Captain, he's a fine man, sir—a super man."

Staff Sergeant Carpenter, his face all scrunched up again and looking down at Sergeant Roebuck, says, "A super man?"

The words seem to linger in the room a moment. Staff Sergeant Carpenter and Sergeant Roebuck realize that Captain Jones and Gunnery Sergeant Morehouse are looking at them, and the gunnery sergeant's look is pure disgust.

"I don't know," says Gunnery Sergeant Morehouse, breaking the silence and shaking his head. "There's something hinky about this one, Captain."

"You're right, Gunny. Probably another spy from division. Get rid of 'im," says Captain Jones.

"We'll do our job, Captain," says Senior Drill Instructor Gunnery Sergeant Morehouse with an air of defiance.

"Good," says Captain Jones sharply. "I still think you have a good shot this time in the drill competition. I've seen your guys drilling. They are not completely retarded. That guide—he doesn't suck too badly."

"Any time frame on the piss test results?" asks Gunnery Sergeant Morehouse.

"Should be soon, Gunny. I'll let you know." The captain turns to leave the office, but then he turns again and says, "Why? Should you be worried, Gunny?"

"Oh, me? No, I'm good," says Gunnery Sergeant Morehouse. "But Sergeant Roebuck here, he's a lil' bit nervous."

"Ha ha ha ha ha ha ha ha aha! He's joking, sir," says Drill Instructor Sergeant Roebuck, clearing his throat and looking uncomfortable with such an unwarrantable smear of his reputation. Gunny Morehouse smiles and shakes his head.

"That's all for now," says the captain.

"Attention on deck!" says Gunnery Sergeant Morehouse. The three drill instructors snap from parade rest to attention.

The captain strides out of the office, heading for the stairwell. A recruit coming out of the head stops dead in his tacks, goes to attention like a board, and shouts, "Attention on deck!"

All the recruits again jump to attention; however, now all the recruits are on line in front of their footlockers. The platoon realizes that lights–out cannot be far away. Captain Jones turns and strides back to the quarterdeck. He stands athwart the enormous Marine Corps insignia painted on the red concrete quarterdeck.

"Marines, get a good night of rest tonight; you'll need it here more than ever," says the captain thoughtfully. "And let's see ... make yourself eat everything they give you at the mess hall or MRE when you're out in the field. You will need all the calories you get here, and it still won't be enough, I promise you. And okay, let's see, I never do this," says the captain, taking a quick moment to recognize the platoon. "Never fall asleep on fire watch! Stay diligent, men! My staff is everywhere, and they are freakin' insomniacs, and they will freakin' constantly be patrolling the barracks buildings and grounds at night and will be challenging you on your knowledge. Be ready! Study your green monsters! And trust the freakin' marines! At ease and good night, Marines!" Captain Jones turns and strides down the passageway beyond the stairwell portal.

There are a few moments of complete silence and no movement. Then, slowly, the squad bay begins to buzz with quiet drilling, and some recruits sit on their footlockers to read or write. Teneriffe again begins to read in his green monster, trying to memorize the information enclosed, but there is also something therapeutic to Teneriffe in just the act of reading. It relaxes him, and it serves as a comfort and an escape into the lightness of his imagination.

"Ten seconds till lights-out!" sings Drill Instructor Staff Sergeant Carpenter as he comes flying out of the office's doorway.

"Discipline, sir, discipline, d-i-s-c-i-p-l-i-n-e ..."

TENERIFFE LIES IN HIS RACK awake. He listens to the slow, steady breathing of the other recruits sleeping. It has to be close to reveille, but ever since the first few mornings when the drill instructors used clanging trash can lids to awaken the recruits, Teneriffe gets up on his own before the morning calamity begins. Teneriffe, from his top rack, props himself up on his elbows and sees another recruit across the squad bay on the port side silently slip out of his rack and start to put on his olive-drab socks, kneeling down between the racks.

Teneriffe sees the recruit look up at him, and the recruit says in a whisper, "Are you okay?"

Huh? Teneriffe nods. "Yeah," Teneriffe says in a whisper. It's a strange question, and it somewhat perplexes Teneriffe. *Why wouldn't I be okay?* Yet, lately, Ten has a peculiar feeling the other recruits are looking at him on line in the morning.

Just then, Staff Sergeant Carpenter comes dashing confidently out of the drill instructor's office. The drill instructors no longer use trash can lids to sound reveille.

Still, they do shout and sing as they trumpet the beginning of the training day.

The staff sergeant flips on the banks of light switches. "Wake up, you beauties! No more dreaming of your little sweet bums! Jodi's spoonin' your girl now anyways!"

The recruits jump in line and stand at attention in their white skivvy shorts and their green skivvy T-shirts. Teneriffe sees Staff Sergeant Carpenter quickly reverse his momentum and reenter the office, having momentarily forgotten something. Teneriffe realizes uncomfortably that the other guys are staring in his general direction.

What the freak is everybody lookin' at?

He looks at the other recruits with sleep in his eyes and confusion. Then Teneriffe holds his hands out, palms up, and says under his breath, "What ... sorry!"

Some recruits shake their heads, and some of them chuckle. The recruit next to Teneriffe in line, Cookie Jarvis, says, "You were shouting and cussing in your sleep last night."

"What, really? No way. Well, crap, I don't think I can do anything about that," whispers Teneriffe.

Drill Instructor Staff Sergeant Carpenter again comes storming out of the office, and all the recruits are back at attention, heads and eyes straight ahead.

Staff Sergeant Carpenter yells, "Socks! Yuns got ten..." All the recruits grab their green socks and begin to dress themselves as the whole platoon again counts down from ten.

"Ten, nine, eight, seven, six, five, four, three, two, one, freeze, Private, freeze!" screams the whole platoon.

"Okay, who doesn't have their socks on yet? Let's see ... Tenegrief, super!" Staff Sergeant Carpenter strides down the center of the squad bay looking at the recruits' feet. "What's the matter, First Squad Leader, too many dreams about your little baby girl got you off this morning? And what do we have here? Private Hay Fly as well can't get his friggin' socks on, as usual. That's no freakin' surprise. Tenegrief, Hay Fly! Up on my quarterdeck now! Move!"

Teneriffe and Hay Fly run up to the quarterdeck.

Staff Sergeant Carpenter commands, "Bend and reach, now move!"

The two recruits begin exercising and count in four count, cadence count. Teneriffe shouts while jumping down to the ground, kicking his feet out, bringing his feet back and again rising to attention, "One, two, three, one; one, two, three, two; one, two, three, three ..." Hay Fly too begins to shout out the cadence count.

After twenty-five repetitions, Staff Sergeant Carpenter yells, "Get off my freakin' quarterdeck now! Move!"

The two recruits stand at attention in their skivvies with only one sock on apiece, sweating and panting. Teneriffe yells between heavy breaths, "Sir, get off the quarterdeck, aye, sir!" Both recruits quickly run back to the line.

"Let's add something new," says Staff Sergeant Carpenter, grinning. "Whenever anybody goes to the quarterdeck, he will be joined by his squad leader. That should get it going around here." Staff Sergeant Carpenter smiles and nods at Sergeant Roebuck, who has joined along in the morning training schedule. Sergeant Roebuck fluctuates between a smile and a look like he wants to swat you in the head. Meanwhile, the recruits continue to dress by the numbers. Occasionally, a recruit does not make the ten-second time limit for donning an article of his uniform and is summoned to the quarterdeck for corporal punishment. The second time Hay Fly doesn't meet his deadline, he and the Fourth Squad leader run to the quarterdeck.

"Wait a second!" yells Staff Sergeant Carpenter. "Wait a second! Hell no! I got another great idea this morning. Wait a second. I think the captain might have to give me my own platoon soon. Hay Fly, you're now in First Squad with Tenegrief! Do you hear me, Tenegrief?"

"Aye, Drill Instructor Staff Sergeant Carpenter!" says Teneriffe as he double-times up to the quarterdeck.

"Get the hell off my quarterdeck, Fourth Squad Leader!"

The Fourth Squad leader hurriedly vacates the quarterdeck and is replaced by Teneriffe.

"Push-ups, ready position, move!"

After all the recruits are back in line and fully dressed, finally, Staff Sergeant Carpenter addresses the platoon again. "Okay, Recruits, you've got fifteen minutes until morning chow, so break up into your squads and turn to morning cleanup. Squad leaders, you've got your assignments, now move!"

All the recruits scramble in a mad dash to their assigned duties. One squad sweeps the squad bay floor using only their dry scrub brushes. They start along the edge of the bulkhead and then crawl along on their hands and knees, brushing toward the center of the squad bay.

When all the dust and dirt has been pushed into a long line in the center of the room, one recruit sweeps down the middle with a long push broom.

First Squad turns to the head for cleanup detail. Teneriffe assigns the recruits different tasks. He delegates some recruits to clean the toilets, some to do the sinks and mirrors, and some to do the shower bulkheads. One recruit sweeps, and another swabs the deck behind him. Teneriffe goes around shouting encouragement to the cleanup detail.

"Let's go, you beauties! Jodi might have our girls now, but the way to a lady's heart is a clean head. Believe me, y'all, Jodi can't make a toilet sparkle like we can! Hay Fly! What are you doin'? Give me that rag." Teneriffe takes the rag from Hay Fly and begins to scrub the white porcelain toilet base. "Like this, Hay Fly. You've got to scrub and then wipe, and you've got to move fast, see?"

"Tenegrief!" shouts the guide, entering the head.

"What? We're busy working!" shouts Teneriffe, scrubbing toilets with Hay Fly.

"DIs want to see you in their office ASAP!"

"Uh oh," says Hay Fly.

"Keep up the … uh … good work, men." *Don't be corny.*

Teneriffe leaves the head and is at the yellow handprint. *One, two, three, four, five.* "Sir, Recruit Teneriffe requests permission to enter the drill instructors' office, sir!"

"Get the hell in here, Tenegrief! Are you trying to knock down my freakin' walls?" asks Senior Drill Instructor Gunnery Sergeant Morehouse, disgusted.

"Sir, aye, sir!" shouts Teneriffe, beaming.

"Well, knock it the freak off," the gunny says, seriously disgusted. "Look, First Squad Leader, we want the names of recruits in your squad that aren't pulling their weight. You haven't given us one name yet. Now look, either you've got the best squad in Parris Island history, or you're not doin' your freakin' job. So give us a list of names. Got it, Tenegrief?"

Are they serious? This is a test, right?

"Yeah, First Squad Leader! Ya know what? Ya wanna know something fascinating?" says Sergeant Roebuck with a stitched lip and a mean countenance.

"Yeah, ya wanna know something mind-blowing, First Squad Leader?" says Staff Sergeant Carpenter as he mimics an explosion with his giant fists on either side of his temples out into the atmosphere.

"The Second Squad leader gives us names," spits Sergeant Roebuck.

"Whoa! No way! Can you freakin' believe that shit? And guess what else, First Squad Leader Tenegrief?" says Staff Sergeant Carpenter.

"The Third Squad leader gives us names," spits Sergeant Roebuck.

"Whoa, Nellie! Oh my freakin' Gawd! Can you freakin' believe that shit? Third Squad leader gives us names, Second Squad leader gives us names, and I wonder who the freak else gives us names besides *not* our freakin' First Squad Leader Tenegrief?" says Staff Sergeant Carpenter.

"Freakin' Fourth Squad leader gives us a freakin' ton of freakin' names!" says Sergeant Roebuck.

"Jesus H. Christ! Fourth Squad leader gives up tons of names! Fourth Squad leader would turn his freakin' mother in. But guess who gives us the most names of anybody?" says Staff Sergeant Carpenter.

"Yeah, Tenegrief, go ahead and guess. Guess who gives us by far and away the most names, and you don't give us shit! Go ahead and guess," says Sergeant Roebuck.

"The guide," says Gunnery Sergeant Morehouse, sitting behind his desk. "That's right, Tenegrief, the guide gives us names too, lots of names, and who the freak knows, First Squad Leader, your name might be on one of those lists already. So listen the freak up! We want freakin' names of anybody not pulling their weight during work assignments or any other freakin' time! Got it? Good! Now get the freak out of my office!"

"Dismissed, aye, sir!" *Ha. I ain't no snitch.*

Teneriffe is back in the head in a moment to see all the recruits finished and standing around talking. "What did they want?" asks Hay Fly. All the recruits are listening.

"They want a list of names of recruits that are slacking on work detail."

Some of the recruits laugh nervously.

Teneriffe smiles and looks at all the recruits in First Squad. "I told 'em I'm leading the greatest squad in Parris Island history! The leanest, meanest, heartbreakin'est, life takin'est, head cleaningest sons of bitches, and if I did give them names, they would probably gut me like a fish in my rack in the middle of the night! What are they gonna do? Shave my head and send me to freakin' boot camp?"

"Get on line!" bellows Staff Sergeant Carpenter from the quarterdeck. "Yuns got ten …"

Love Marine and Love terrene—
Love celestial too—

—Emily Dickinson

Sppt! A round rips the paper target above the heads of the recruits standing in the butts. Teneriffe and the Second Squad leader, a tall recruit that the other recruits just call Bubba, pull down the silver-painted iron frame that holds the large white target with a black silhouette of a man's torso for the bull's-eye. The whole white paper target is about eight feet tall and four feet wide, but from five hundred yards away, it is barely the size of the rifle's front sight post.

"'Nother bull's-eye!" says Bubba as he jams the cardboard disk, white side out, into the bullet hole. "This guy's dingin' it!"

Both the recruits hoist the target up again using the iron handles on the sides of the frame. Teneriffe grabs the spotter, a metal disk about the size of a personal pizza attached to a long wooden pole painted red on one side and white on the other. He lifts the spotter pole and covers the black, revealing that this shooter has hit another bull's-eye. Then the two recruits pull down the target again. Bubba patches the bullet hole that has ripped through the target with a black sticker.

"Holy shit!" says Bubba, "This feller is really whoopin' the shit out of it!"

Then the two quickly raise the patched target up into the dangerous air above the protective earth berm once more.

"We're gonna run out of black stickers," says Teneriffe, plopping back down on the wooden bench.

It's a beautiful day. The sky is blue, with large, billowy white clouds. The recruits sit on wooden benches or stand on the concrete gangway looking out into the ocean that serves as the impact area. This is one of the first times that the recruits have not been under immediate supervision by the drill instructors, resulting in a very pleasant and relaxed environment. The butts are protected by an earth berm reinforced with concrete, which provides a nice cool shade as well.

Today is qualification day, the last day of a two-week period that the recruits have spent at the rifle range. The first week at the range was spent in classroom learning basic rifle marksmanship. A PMI (primary marksmanship instructor) coached the platoon on everything they needed to know about firing their weapons. Among the marksmanship lessons were breath control, trigger control, sight adjusting, windage, battle sight zero, sighting in, and the distance and positions that they would be qualifying on the range with the M16A2 service rifle.

Many of the recruits talk about becoming a PMI someday in hushed tones, like it would be like hitting the lottery. The PMI commands the respect of the DIs but seems cooler and somewhat closer in age to the recruits, and the job entails living on a live-fire KD course training, qualifying, and practicing with different units that continually cycle into your instruction. Teneriffe's PMI has a tattoo of a man's face on his upper arm that has been cut into rectangles, and the rectangles are slightly moved out of place, giving the face a distorted appearance. Under the picture are the words, "Life is pain, I wish to be insane."

A lot of this first week on the range is called snapping in. The platoon is spaced out into a giant circle surrounding a big white metal barrel that has black spots painted on its sides. The platoon snaps in or sights in on the white barrel in one of four shooting positions for hours, and the platoon does this every day for the first week. There is the standing firing position, the kneeling firing position, the sitting firing position, and the prone firing position.

In the standing firing position, the marine stands with the rifle stock against his or her cheek, supporting the full weight of the rifle with his or her arms and shoulders. The rifle sling is either tight with no slack against the rifle, which is called tight parade sling, or taken off the rifle completely. Standing for a long period of time in this position can be somewhat painful. The shoulders get fatigued very quickly. In the following months and years out in the fleet, a favorite punishment and form of physical training is for the marine to hold his or her weapon out away from the body, strengthening the deltoid muscles, while running or standing in formation.

The most stable position for shooting is the prone firing position. The marine lies on the ground on his or her belly, supporting the rifle with his or her elbows on the ground. The sling is tightly rigged around the shooter's bicep. Although the arm can sometimes become numb from the sling constricting blood flow, this position is the most comfortable and easy to maintain throughout the hours of sighting in. Unfortunately, the PMI doesn't allow the platoon to stay in this position for very long, lest someone get some rest.

Next is the seated firing position. The shooter sits Indian style on the ground with the shooter's sling slung around his or her bicep. Imagine sitting Indian style for an hour, hunched over, with your elbows in the hollow of your knees and your neck twisted and cheek mashed up against the butt of your rifle. Now imagine the headache of scrunching your brow and squinting one eye closed, focusing your vision on a white polka-dotted barrel through the sight posts of your rifle, and you may begin to understand the pain of the marine recruit.

The last firing position is the kneeling position. Some recruits are so flexible that they actually sit on a foot turned sideways like the green plastic army men. Again, the sling is around the shooter's bicep muscle so that the rifle is supported and sturdier. Imagine now that you're sitting on your foot turned sideways and your lead leg is flexed with your elbow perched on top of the flexed knee. Your neck is twisted, and your face is smashed up against the rifle butt. The forehead and eyes must again perform their telescopic duty through the fatigue and salty sweat. The benefit of this variant is that the front leg does not have to flex as severely to become the shooter's table. The other variant of the kneeling firing position, and the more painful one because both knees must be flexed tightly, is to kneel on the ground with your rear foot flexed and toes in contact with the ground as you flex your front knee and use it as the shooter's perch. Either way, a few hours in the kneeling firing position is quite painful, and it's the one the PMI loves to keep the platoon in for hours.

"Life is pain, I wish to be insane."

"What did you qualify as, Bubba?" asks Teneriffe.

"Oh, I made rifle expert no problem," replies Bubba. "I've been shootin' since before I could walk. Dad would take us huntin' every weekend during huntin' season."

There are three classifications for the rifle qual in the United States Marine Corps, and every marine wears a metal badge on his or her dress uniform that tells everyone in the world which class he or she qualified as. The three classes are, from highest to lowest, rifle expert, rifle sharpshooter, and rifle marksman.

"I only made sharpshooter," says Teneriffe. "It ain't like shootin' baskets back home, for sure. That's what my brothers and I used to do all summer long. That and go to the pool."

"We'd go to the lake," says Bubba. "I miss it fiercely, son. Boy, how we used to sun out by the lake catchin' fish or skiing. Hey, Ten, ain't it funny how you only miss a thing when it's gone?"

"I hear that, Bubba. Hey, what made you join the Marine Corps, anyways?" asks Teneriffe.

Bubba is standing and leaning on the iron framework that holds the target in the air. His chest is against an iron bar, and his arms dangle over the iron metalwork. Bubba is about six three and blond when he has hair. He is looking up at the target and the blue sky above as large, billowy white clouds sail slowly along, and he says slowly and quietly, "Oh, I always wanted to be a marine." The air is still, and everyone in the butts seems to be listening. "I guess I always knew I'd become one, a marine. Dad used to have me in dress blues when I was still a young'un 'bout four or five. But ya know what, Ten? I just couldn't bring myself to go to the recruiter's office and enlist. I just couldn't do it. I was havin' too much fun after high school and enjoying life too damned much. Then, of course, Momma died."

Sppt! Another round rips through the air above them. Bubba steps back, and he and Teneriffe pull down the target using the big iron handles attached to the iron frame. The target frame is heavy, and just pulling down the target and hoisting it back into the air is a workout.

"'Nother bull's-eye!" shouts Bubba.

All the other recruits in the butts manning the targets near Teneriffe and Bubba are beginning to take notice. Teneriffe marks the score on a scorecard.

Bubba asks, "They're on the five hundred yard line, right?"

"Sure are. Only two more bull's-eyes and this dude's got himself a perfect score."

"No way!" says another recruit close by.

"Really?" says another. "Radical!"

Marines pride themselves on their rifle shooting. Every marine, whether a cook or a recon ranger, must qualify every year on the KD course. KD stands for known distance, and the marines take it very seriously. The qualifying on the last day involves five stages of fire. Stage one is at two hundred yards. The marines have twenty minutes to squeeze off fifteen rounds, which is called slow fire. The first five rounds are taken from the seated firing position. The next five rounds are from the kneeling firing position, and the last five are in the standing firing position.

The second stage is a rapid-fire test performed in seventy seconds. The marine fires five rounds in the standing firing position with one magazine. Then the marine must change magazines and fire off the remaining five rounds from the kneeling firing position.

Stage three and four are from the three hundred yard line. The marine fires another five rounds in a slow-fire exercise in the kneeling position. Stage four is the same as the rapid fire in stage two, but it is performed from the greater distance.

The last stage of the rifle qualification is a ten-round slow fire from five hundred yards in the prone firing position for ten minutes.

"Well, anyways, like I said, Momma died, and I was really down in the dumps for a long time. Everything back home changed directly; everywhere I looked reminded me of her and how much I missed her. Well, so finally, after all, I decided to enlist, like I always knew I would. But I'll tell you the really funny thing, Ten. I've come halfway across this country, right, all this way, and I feel her with me more than ever. I feel her presence all around me—all around us—right now! She's there in the clouds; that's her smile. Look there in the little curl of the waves that are playing on the surface of the water there. That's Momma!"

All the recruits nearby in the butts are listening and looking around in wonder.

"You're freakin' nuts," says Private Royals with a sneer.

"I *am* freakin' nuts," replies Bubba, "but it's still true, I tell you. I feel it true in my heart, and it has kept me happy even in this freakin' crazy-ass place."

The unsupervised boots look to everything around them. "And the birds there in the sky, and the fishes underneath the water—they are Momma too."

"How 'bout Staff Sergeant Carpenter? Is he Momma too?" asks Private Royals in a mocking hick voice.

"Oh, no!" says Bubba. "Staff Sergeant Carpenter is positively not Momma."

The marines all laugh.

"I actually heard her voice speak to me the first day of snap-in week. Remember, Ten, the first day here at the range, we ate breakfast like at zero three thirty or something, and we were waiting outside the mess hall in the dark before breakfast waiting for all the other platoons to file in for chow. We were the last ones to go in, as usual. Well, I was looking up and kind of staring at that big ol' full moon, and I heard Momma's voice in my ear say that she was proud of me for comin' all this way and all."

"You are freakin' bat-shit crazy," says Private Royals.

"I *am* freakin' crazy," replies Bubba, "but it's the God's honest truth that I heard Momma's voice sure as I'm standing right here with all you morons. No offense, Ten."

"Oh, none taken, Bubba," says Teneriffe with a chuckle and a roll of his eyes.

Sppt! The round rips the paper target above their heads, and the two boys pull down the target.

"Bull's-eye!" yells Bubba.

"No way," says a recruit nearby.

"Unreal," says another. "Totally awesome!"

A recruit walks down the concrete gangway in the butts handing out supplies. "You guys need more stickers?"

"Yeah, we need more stickers, especially black ones; this dude is rippin' it up there," says Teneriffe. He and Bubba again work the butts, pulling and heaving, patching and spotting. The recruit gives them a new roll of white stickers and a new roll of black stickers, which Teneriffe puts down on the wooden bench.

"Oh, guess what," says the recruit. "We're spotting for a platoon of WMs."

WM is short for woman marine.

"No way!" shouts Bubba, who then jumps up and grabs the top of the overhead concrete berm with two hands and does a pull-up so it appears he is sticking his head over the berm to see the girls downrange. Thankfully, Bubba is not in danger, because the grass and dirt part of the berm rises several feet above the concrete reinforcement, but it still looks funny.

"You're an idiot, Bubba," laughs Private Royals.

All the marines close enough laugh at Bubba. Then Bubba lets go and drops back to the concrete gangway.

"See, that's Momma too! Momma does have a sense of humor, don't she?" Bubba says with a broad smile across his face. His feet are spread apart, and his arms hang along the side of his thick, muscular body. Bubba exudes a natural charisma.

Sppt! The final round rips the paper target above their heads. Bubba and Teneriffe pull down the target.

"Bull's-eye!"

A few days after qualifying on the rifle range, back at Third Battalion in their home barracks, Hay Fly and Teneriffe are making their racks together one morning.

"How many times do you think we were on the quarterdeck yesterday?" asks Hay Fly.

"It must have been about thirty times," says Teneriffe. He looks at Hay Fly in disgust.

"I'm sorry," says Hay Fly.

"It's just games. Besides, I'm in the best shape of my life!" says Teneriffe looking on the bright side of things and trying to bolster Hay Fly's confidence.

"I know, Ten. Carpenter threw you off the quarterdeck the last three times because you were like a friggin' machine," says Hay Fly.

The recruits are putting hospital corners on the bottom rack.

"Where did you learn to shoot so well?" asks Teneriffe.

"I don't know. It just comes naturally, I guess," says Hay Fly with a shrug of his shoulders.

"Nobody could freakin' believe it. High score in the battalion—unbelievable," says Teneriffe.

Hay Fly beams a giant, gap-toothed smile.

"If it weren't for that woman marine, I would have had high score in the regiment," adds Hay Fly dreamily.

"I know. Unbelievable. I was on her target, ya know. Yeah! When we found out she was a WM, Higginson wanted us to mess with the scoring, but Bubba and I wouldn't have nothin' to do with it. Bubba kept sayin', 'Not in front of Momma, no way, no way.' Can you imagine a girl shooting an M16 like that? I mean wow! Now that's a dangerous weapon, a woman that can shoot a rifle with that kind of accuracy," says Teneriffe.

"She didn't miss any bull's-eyes. I missed three," says Hay Fly.

"Anyway, it's prestigious as hell what you did on the range," says Teneriffe.

"I still won't be able to put my socks on in ten seconds," laughs Hay Fly.

"I know," says Teneriffe. "Me neither. The first day I'm home, I'm gonna take fifteen minutes to put on my freakin' shoes and socks."

Teneriffe then thinks about some advice to maybe help Hay Fly. "I have noticed, though, a lot of recruits are sleeping with their socks on or waking up early and putting them on before reveille. Why don't you try that?" says Teneriffe, thinking about the recruit he saw some days ago doing just that.

"Hey, Ten, ya think we'll make it to the fleet?"

"Piece of cake," says Teneriffe.

'Tis good—the looking back on Grief—
—Emily Dickinson

"YOU'RE A FREAKING LYING SACK of shit!" yells the battalion adjutant with a gold oak leaf on either collar. "My God! I can't believe my freakin' goddamn ears! I can't even stand to look at you! You ... you ... you freaked up monkey freaker! You're not worth the jizz on your daddy's trousers, boy! You're a pile of monkey spunk! You're lower than maggot shit! You're the lowest low-life scumbag I've ever laid my sorry eyes on! I can't believe what a freakin' asshole you are! Are you freakin' retarded? Are you? Answer me! You'd better tell me the freakin' truth, and I mean right freakin' now, Private ... Private ..." The major looks down at the brown folder in front of him. "Teneriffe!"

About an hour earlier, five recruits were called into their drill instructors' office on the third floor of their redbrick barracks building. In the office, Teneriffe and four other recruits were astonished to see Gunnery Sergeant Morehouse remove his Smokey Bear cover and speak to them like normal human beings for the first time since they arrived at the recruit training depot.

"You men have been identified as having your urinalysis testing come back positive for drugs," said Gunnery Sergeant Morehouse, looking down at the deck. The senior drill instructor looked up and said, "Tenegrief, when I dismiss you, I want you to march this detail to the battalion adjutant's office across the parade ground. Now, no grab assin' or bullshittin'."

That was when he looked at the detail for the first time without disgust and contempt and said plainly, conversationally, "Do you have any questions for me?" The gunnery sergeant sighed audibly and lowered his eyes to the olive-drab desk. One fist sat on the desk, and the other rested on his hip.

At first there was complete silence in the small, overcrowded room. The five boys kind of looked around at each other in disbelief.

"Sir, I have a drug waiver, sir," said one recruit.

"Sir, I have one too, sir."

"Sir, me too, sir," said another.

"Wait, now listen," said Gunnery Sergeant Morehouse, holding up one palm. "Just go down to the battalion adjutant's office over there in battalion headquarters and look them in the eye and tell them the truth. That's all you can do. They *cannot* take away from you the fine work you have put in during these weeks of basic training."

Then one of the recruits asked, "Sir, how many recruits were positive for drugs in your last platoon, sir?"

"Oh, that's a good question. Let's see," said Gunnery Sergeant Morehouse. "Actually, this is a very good class. Last platoon had eight recruits come up positive, five for marijuana and three for cocaine, and the class before that one had ten recruits come up positive for mostly marijuana but two for cocaine. You all were just positive for marijuana, and there's only five of you."

All the young recruits looked around pleased and smiled and nodded at each other.

Then the same recruit asked, "Sir, how many of them got sent home, sir?"

Gunnery Sergeant Morehouse, looking at Teneriffe, said, "All of 'em. Everybody that comes up positive on the drug test gets sent home."

Another recruit said in a faltering voice, "Sir, but I'm a drug waiver, sir."

"Okay. Hold on, guys. Tenegrief, I want you to march this detail over to battalion. Dismissed!"

"Detail, fall out in the passageway," ordered Teneriffe.

The detail marched down the stairwell, formed up outside, and marched across the sun-drenched parade ground that separated the barracks buildings from the battalion headquarters.

All along the way, the recruits marched on the black tar surface in silence until one of the recruits finally cheered up and said, "Well, I guess it's over, guys. This is a fucked up way to be sent home, though."

"Well, shit, fellas, we'll be home soon," said one recruit.

"Hell yeah!" said another. "Thank God, we won't have to put up with any more of these fucked up games and all this other fuckin' bullshit. I mean fuck this shit, right? They just want fuckin' bodies; am I right?"

"Hell yeah, motherfuckers. I am fuckin' done!" said another soon-to-be-separated recruit. "I mean the first time one of those jive ass dick wads jumped up and shouted in my face, I should have socked 'em right in their fuckin' face!"

"I know! What the hell?" said one of the others. "Haven't they ever just thought of asking someone to do something nicely?"

"Right, right," laughed another. "You know, *please* and *thank you* go a long way in my book. Like, 'Hey, man, pass me another beer, please.'"

The guys laughed, except for Teneriffe.

"Dudes, dudes, I'm gonna get *so* drunk. Then I'm gonna hook up with my girlfriend and her friends, and dudes, check it out, I'm gonna get me some fuckin' *pizza* first thing, dudes!"

"Yeah! Some 'za!"

"I'm gonna have a big ass pizza too and get *so* wasted!"

"I'm going to have a large pizza too with everything on it. Deep dish," said the last recruit. "Pepperoni, sausage, onions, green peppers, olives, ham, ground beef, mushrooms, pineapples …"

As they neared the entrance of the battalion headquarters, Teneriffe said, "All right, let's hold it down, now."

One recruit who had already begun to relish the freedom of his soon-to-be-civilian status said, "Lighten up Tenegrief. It's over!"

"Yeah, awright," said Teneriffe, who waited last in line outside the battalion adjutant's office portal.

Each recruit went in and then came out and was gone. When the last recruit before him went in, Teneriffe listened to the conversation from around the side of the bulkhead.

"Your urinalysis has come back positive for marijuana. Did you smoke or ingest any marijuana in the last few weeks or months?" asked the battalion adjutant.

The recruit explained how his friends had given him a going-away keg party where large amounts of alcohol were consumed, and although he could not be sure, the recruit thought he might have smoked a little grass in his very drunken, almost unconscious state.

"Very good," said the major. "You are to go back to your platoon, pack up your gear in your sea bag, and report back to this battalion office to be driven to a separation platoon, where you will be for ten to twenty days before being sent home. Now get the freak out of here, but be back as soon as possible. *Next!*"

Teneriffe entered the small office and came to attention about three feet in front of the major's desk. "Sir, Recruit Teneriffe reporting as ordered, sir."

"At ease, Recruit," said the major with a little curl of his lip.

Teneriffe cut sharply from attention to parade rest but kept his vision like a laser beam on a spot on the wall about two feet above the major's head.

"Your urinalysis has come back positive for marijuana. Did you smoke or ingest any marijuana in the last few weeks or months?"

"Sir, yes, sir. This recruit smoked some marijuana eight months ago for experimental purposes as signed and sworn to in my paperwork, sir."

"No, no, no," said the major, shaking his head. "I can see that you are a drug waiver from eight months ago. What I'm asking is if you have done marijuana since then."

"Sir, no, sir!"

"No! Come on, Recruit. You and I know the test don't lie. When was the last time you used marijuana?"

"Sir, I've only smoked marijuana once in my life, and that was eight months ago and documented in my packet, sir!"

"Wait! Wha ... what the freak!" The major jumped up out of his chair and slapped the desktop with both his palms. That was when he started his tirade.

"You're a freaking lying sack of shit! My God! I can't believe my freakin' goddamn ears! I can't even stand to look at you! You ... you ... you freaked up monkey freaker! You're not worth the jizz on your daddy's trousers, son! You're a pile of monkey spunk! You're lower than maggot shit! You're the lowest low-life scumbag I've ever laid my sorry eyes on! I can't believe what a freakin' asshole you are! Are you freakin' retarded? Well, are you? Answer me! You'd better tell me the freakin' truth, and I mean right freakin' now, Private ... Private ..." The major looks down at the brown folder in front of him. "Teneriffe! Did you take marijuana before coming here in addition to the time eight months prior?"

"Sir, no, sir!"

The major is livid and begins to rant. "Our test isn't wrong, dumbass—you're wrong! And it says you're positive for marijuana. Furthermore, we know and you know that a joint from eight months ago would not produce a positive result on any goddamn drug test at recruit training!" The major is speaking very quickly. "So you had better come clean and tell the truth, Private, and I mean right freakin' now! Did you smoke or ingest marijuana since your drug waiver of eight months ago!"

"Sir, no, sir! There must be something wrong with the test results."

"Bullshit!" thunders the major so loudly that the battalion passageway seems to echo the word back. "You are in serious trouble, Marine, so you better tell me the freakin' truth, and I mean it. Our test is never wrong. You're the one that's freakin' wrong!"

A particularly large and muscled staff sergeant passing by the office entrance sticks his head in. "Is everything okay here, Major?"

"Staff Sergeant, come in here. You've got to hear this bullshit. I can't believe my freakin' goddamn ears." The staff sergeant comes in and gets about an inch from the right side of Teneriffe's face.

"Recruit, uh-ten-huh!" commands the staff sergeant.

Teneriffe snaps to attention, keeping his eyes fixed on the spot on the wall.

The staff sergeant blasts into Teneriffe's ear, spit sprinkling the side of his face and the brim of the staff sergeant's felt Smokey Bear cover rubbing Teneriffe's temple, "You're in big freakin' trouble, Recruit, if you keep with this disgusting, horrible, freaked up lie of yours.

We know that the test results are always correct, and we know that positive results only show up for regular, recent, and long-term use of drugs! So we are absolutely sure you're a freakin' low-life scumbag liar and a piece of shit, pothead! All we want to hear from you now is the freakin' goddamn truth! You smoked pot, didn't you! Didn't you!"

"Sir, no, sir!"

"Jesus freakin' Christ, Major, can you believe this freakin' guy? Major, please let me take him out back and beat the truth out of this freakin' asshole," shouts the staff sergeant, balling Teneriffe's collar in his fist.

"You better tell us the truth, asshole. I'm gonna ask you again, and you better come up with the correct answer, or you know what? I'm definitely gonna let the staff sergeant here take you out back and do what he wants to do to you," says the major. "Did you smoke or ingest marijuana other than the time in your bullshit drug waiver!"

"Sir, no, sir!"

"No!" says the major. "No! No! No! Oh, what freakin' bullshit! You're freakin' gone, all right! It's just gonna take a little longer to squeeze the truth out of this shit bag! But we will get the freakin' truth out of you, shit bird! Oh, believe me, we will get the truth! One way or another, we will get to the freakin' truth!"

"Recruit Teneriffe, you're to report back to your platoon for now, but don't get too freakin' comfortable, asshole! You're absolutely freakin' gone one way or another, shithead, and I mean for good! Dismissed, goddamn it!"

"Sir, dismissed, aye, sir!"

BACK IN THE DARKNESS OF the squad bay at night, illuminated only by the red signs that mark the exits to the stairwells, Teneriffe and Cookie Jarvis walk on their fire watch. In the dead of the night, they march like toy soldiers up and down the squad bay, passing each other occasionally. The rear portal swings open in a rush, and a strange lieutenant comes striding into the passageway behind the head and the drill instructors' office. He is wearing the duty war belt of the officer of the day.

Teneriffe strides up to meet the lieutenant and salutes with his M16A2. "Nothing to report at this time. All is quiet," reports Teneriffe.

"Good. What's your name, Recruit?" asks the strange lieutenant.

"Sir, Private Teneriffe, sir."

"What's your fourth general order, Private Teneriffe?"

"Sir, this marine's fourth general order is to repeat all calls from posts more distant from the guardhouse than my own."

"What is your fifth general order?"

"Sir, this marine's fifth general order is to quit my post only when … when only properly relieved, sir."

"What is your sixth general order?"

"Sir, this marine's sixth general order is to receive, obey, and pass on to the sentry who relieves me all orders from the commanding officer, officer of the day, and officers and noncommissioned officers of the guard only, sir."

"What are the two sources for the law of war?"

"Sir, the two sources for the law of war are lawmaking treaties and custom, sir."

"Give me two basic principles of the law of war."

"Sir, two basic principles of the law of war are marines fight only enemy combatants, and marines do not kill or torture prisoners, sir."

"What are the purposes of the law of war?"

"Sir, the purposes of the law of war are to protect combatants and noncombatants from unnecessary suffering, to safeguard fundamental human rights of persons who fall into the hands of the enemy, and to help bring peace, sir."

"What is the Marine Corps's motto?"

"Sir, the Marine Corps's motto is semper fidelis."

"What does semper fidelis mean?"

"Sir, semper fidelis means always faithful, sir."

"What rank is three stripes up, three stripes down, with a diamond in the center?"

"Sir, three stripes up, three stripes down, and a diamond in the center is a first sergeant, sir."

"What is the rank of three stripes up, three stripes down, and crossed rifles in the center?"

"Sir, the rank of three stripes up, three stripes down, and crossed rifles in the center is a master sergeant, sir."

"What rank is three stripes up, four stripes down, and a star in the center?"

"Sir, the rank of three stripes up, four stripes down, and a star in the center is a sergeant major, sir."

"What is the rank of three stripes up, four stripes down, and a bursting bomb in the center?"

"Sir, the rank of three stripes up, four stripes down, and a bursting bomb in the center is a master gunnery sergeant, sir."

"What is the rank of two stripes up over crossed rifles?"

"Sir, the rank of two stripes up over crossed rifles is a corporal, sir."

"What is the rank of an officer that wears two connected bars?"

"Sir, the rank of an officer that wears two connected bars is a captain, sir."

"How many stars does a major general wear?"

"Sir, a major general wears two stars, sir."

"Who is our commander in chief?"

"Sir, our commander in chief is the president of the United States, sir."

"In the navy, what is the rank of someone that wears an eagle insignia on their collar?"

"Sir, in the navy, a captain wears an eagle insignia, sir," says Teneriffe.

"What is his equal rank in the Marine Corps?"

"Sir, a captain in the navy is equal in rank to a colonel in the Marine Corps, sir."

"What rank is three stripes up, four stripes down, with a Marine Corps insignia inside the center?"

"Sir, the sergeant major of the Marine Corps wears three stripes up, four stripes down, and a Marine Corps insignia inside the center, sir."

"What is deadly force?"

"Sir, deadly force is … sir, deadly force is … sir, this marine does not know the answer at this time but will find out the correct answer as soon as possible, sir. Thank you, sir."

"You're … you're welcome," says the strange lieutenant. "Okay, carry on, fire watch!"

"Carry on, aye, sir," says Teneriffe. With his M16A2 at right shoulder arms, he cuts his left arm horizontally to the rifle sight and back down to his side.

The strange lieutenant disappears into the darkness of the stairwell after returning a sharp solute, and again Cookie Jarvis comes up and smacks the back of Teneriffe's head.

"That was weird," says Cookie Jarvis. "That's the first question you missed."

"I know. What the hell is deadly force? It must have been in that lecture I missed today."

"Need I remind you that I haven't missed a question yet," says Cookie Jarvis with a jovial countenance.

"Yeah, I know, but anyway?"

"I don't know," says Cookie Jarvis. "I imagine we'll find out soon, though. We are training to be marines, right?"

"Yeah, maybe."

"You know they're gonna be coming at you from all different directions now," advises Cookie.

"You mean there are more directions?" says Teneriffe as the two marines sit down on the deck with their backs against the bulkhead.

"Oh yeah! There are many more ways, I assure you. I thought you were a drug waiver, anyway."

"I am, but I'm also a medical waiver. I'm partially blind in one eye," says Teneriffe. "My recruiter didn't think I had a chance at being accepted to the Corps after I failed the eye test at the MEPS center. He told me there was little chance I'd be accepted on a medical, but I guess because I played football and basketball and I was a catcher in baseball my whole dang life, they approved the medical waiver anyways. So the recruiter calls me up one day out of the blue and says that I've been approved on the medical waiver but I have to ship out tomorrow. I told 'im, 'Dude, I ain't exactly been studying for that drug test of y'all's,' and he says not to worry about it."

"What?" says Cookie Jarvis. "Screwed over by a recruiter? No way! Tee hee tee hee hee."

"Yeah, go figure. So apparently even if you were a drug waiver, you still have to have a clean urine sample here at recruit training depot."

"Wow, really? Well, it sucks to be you."

"Tell me about it."

"Tee hee tee hee hee."

"Hey, Ten, why do they call this fire watch? I've walked fire watch so much I can't count the times, and I still haven't seen a fire yet."

"Heard that one already."

"Hee hee hee, I mean the place is made of concrete, for cryin' out loud. Hee hee hee. Wait a sec—heard it already? That's my bit. Is somebody else doin' my material?"

"Right," laughs Teneriffe. "So anyway, they're tellin' me I'm a freakin' liar, they know I'm a freakin' liar, our test don't lie, and you're a low-life scumbag freakin' liar."

"Ouch! That's rough. Anyway, no doubt First Squad is gone, and that's absolutely certain."

Both marines drop their heads and look serious and disappointed.

"I never wanted that shit to begin with," says Teneriffe sadly.

"Hey, Ten, did you notice that staff sergeant in history class today said *freak* or *freakin'* two hundred and fifty-two times during his lecture?" says Cookie, trying to change the subject.

"I had him at two fifty. Does *frick* or *frickin'* count?"

"Yeah, I was countin' *frick* and *frickin'*. He also used *freak* in every part of speech: as a noun, a verb, a pronoun, an adjective, an adverb, a preposition, a conjunction, and an interjection," says Cookie.

"Yeah, right, as a conjunction even. That's pretty impressive. Hey, Cookie, one other thing—help me keep an eye out for the Hay Fly, no matter what happens," says Teneriffe. "The little guy needs our help. At least somebody's gotta be looking out for him."

"Roger that. Tango Charlie?" says Cookie, asking about the time and standing slowly up.

His knees crack and make an awful echo through the rows of sleeping marine recruits snoring or sometimes mumbling confused verses out into the dark concrete coffin.

"Agh, ouch," Cookie grunts as he stands up, tucking his cammy trousers and straightening out his camouflaged blouse.

"You sound like an old maid there, Marine."

"I can still beat your ass in the three-mile run, fat boy."

Fat boy! "Well, it's about that time," says Teneriffe. "It's two fifty-seven."

"Hey, Ten, you wake up Cubano this time. He'll punch you out of a dead sleep when you try to wake him up."

"For real," says Teneriffe. "Maybe he thinks you're a ghost."

"Tee hee tee hee hee. Now that *is* crazy," says Cookie Jarvis, fading back down the long dark corridor. "Tee hee tee hee hee."

"Look, you can relax—Teneriffe, is it? I'm just a regular marine what happens to just work here at the recruit depot. I'm not no drill instructor, and I'm not no officer. So you can drop all this 'Sir, yes, sir!' crap, okay?" says a strange corporal sorting mail in the battalion mailroom. "You don't see no Smokey Bear on my grape, do ya, jarhead?"

"Sir, yes, sir!" yells Teneriffe.

"Okay, whatever, but really we're gonna be here all day sorting mail, and that freakin' yelling is gonna give me a freakin' damned headache, okay? So hold it the freak down, anyway, at least in the battalion headquarters."

Teneriffe and two other recruits have been separated from the normal training schedule and sent to the battalion headquarters for a work detail after morning chow. At battalion, the three recruits were ordered to perform different tasks. The other two privates were detached to a cleaning party, while Teneriffe was assigned to the battalion mailroom to assist a strange corporal with sorting the mail for Third Battalion.

"What's your MOS?" asks the strange corporal. "What are you going to be doing after boot camp?"

"I wanted to be a rifleman, but they put me in a bonus program the recruiter had at the time. He said I could go to a number of different specialties wherever they have a need, and the government would give me a thousand dollars cash bonus," says Teneriffe. "So I said, because rifleman was one of those MOS's on the list, 'Sure, I'll do it!' I mean, it's a thousand bucks, man, Corporal."

"Infantry—wow, that was stupid," says the strange corporal. "Well, at least you've got a chance to do something cool with that bonus program."

"Yeah, they might make me a cook," says Teneriffe sarcastically.

"Yeah, that would really suck," laughs the strange corporal.

"Of course, my friend Cookie says that the marines during the Korean War consisted of mostly cooks and other support personnel that held off the Chinese horde at the famous frozen Chosin Reservoir with valor and distinction the likes of which the world had never seen before and may never know again."

"Yeah, I remember hearing that. So you're really into this Marine Corps history crap, huh?" says the corporal, looking out of the corner of his eye.

"Well, you know, growing up, my friends and I always thought marines were badass fighters, and we, of course, heard a lot of the crazy stories about PI. But ya know, the more history I learn about the marines, the more I want to be one. Like, we learned about the battle of Belleau Wood during World War I. See, the Germans had basically busted through the center of the Allied lines and were fifty miles from Paris with nothing to stop them from goose-stepping into the capitol and winning the war to end all wars. It was just then, like in a movie or something, that two American divisions spearheaded by a brigade of marines came marching up through the wheat fields and forest mist to beat back five German divisions.

"Cookie says that the Fourth Brigade were mainly made up of salty war veterans of the banana wars like Gunnery Sergeant Dan Daly and a bunch of Ivy League volunteers from like Harvard and shit. Well, Cookie says Belleau Wood destroyed German morale and started the legend of the modern Marine Corps. By clearing the woods of Germans in June of 1918, those marines basically tipped the scales in the First World War, leading to an Allied victory. And I mean I'm here now doing the same thing those marines did in basic training. I'm learning the same things they did. I pretty much have got to become a marine now, Corporal. So why did you join the Marine Corps?"

"Really, let's see," the strange corporal says, tapping his index finger on his chin as he looks toward the tiled ceiling with his other hand on his slender hip. "I really never had a physical before. I never had a physical before in my life! I wanted to see what that was all about. While the recruiter was spewing all his other bullshit, I heard him say something about getting a physical at the MEPS Center. So blah, blah, blah, I go get my physical that I'm so jacked up about getting, and well, one thing led to another."

"And how did that physical go for ya?" asks Teneriffe, laughing at the strange corporal's story.

"Really well. I've always been a really fast runner. So, although my MOS is 1811, tanks, I made the Marine Corps long-distance running team. Mostly all I do now is run road races representing the United States Marine Corps."

"Wow, you must be a really good runner. Not me so much."

The strange corporal continues, "Well, there is a lot more good stuff than running long distance. There are a lot of great opportunities in the Marine Corps to play organized athletics. Every command in the US services has intramural sports. Then there are teams that represent the Marine Corps in basketball and softball, running and shooting. And there's all kinds of other stuff too. Check it out. I've got a friend in Twenty-Nine Palms, and all he does all day long is take dependents on horseback riding trails."

"For real? Horseback riding? Dude!"

"Another one of my buddies is actually a lifeguard in Hawaii at the NCO pool. That's all he does is sit in a lifeguard chair and soaks up the rays, dude. And he told me that Lee Travino used to play golf for the Marine Corps in Hawaii too. You know who Lee Travino is? The professional golfer. Well, when he was in the Corps, that's all he did was play golf. That was his MOS. He would go play golf all day long, for cryin' out loud. How about that?"

"Really? No way! Ya know, I met Lee Travino at the Masters one time. Dad took us out of school one year so we could go. Well, Lee Travino is surrounded by a whole gallery of folks in front of Butler Cabin, and he's freakin' crackin' everyone up. He's telling jokes and just talkin' with these fans for like thirty minutes. It was rad. He took pictures with my brothers and me. It was like a show, and he just had everyone in stitches. But I didn't even know he was a marine."

"So what about you, huh? You one of these blood-and-glory types? You wanna be Rambo or something, Tenegrief?"

"Well, it wouldn't suck to win a medal, but I wouldn't say that I'm dreaming of it or anything. I like a chant Drill Instructor Staff Sergeant Carpenter sings when we're running in PT. He says, 'Pray for peace, prepare for war.' I think that about says it for me. Anyway, with the world set in the Cold War, it looks like a decent way to see the world. In fact, Hawaii doesn't sound bad to me at all, but maybe that's the same thing the marines were thinking at Pearl Harbor on December 6, 1941."

The two go back to sorting mail in silence.

"I've heard the smoke in Hawaii is unbelievable," says the strange corporal after a while, breaking the silence.

Now it is Teneriffe that takes a glance out of the corner of his eye. He feels the corporal looking at him.

"You ever get high, Teneriffe? I mean before you joined the Marine Corps? You know, in the fleet it's totally different than here. They maybe piss test you once a year, and even then it's usually tipped off a couple weeks in advance. We all get high every now and then."

"Nope," says Teneriffe.

"Really? You wouldn't believe what we find coming in just in this mail room at recruit training. I swear—some people think this is prison or something. We get loose joints inside letters. We've found blotter acid hidden under stamps."

"Recruits trip at boot camp?"

"I know—talk about a bad trip. We just had a recruit try to fly away off the rooftop of Foxtrot Company's barracks only a few months ago, but his wings didn't work and there wasn't a phantom in sight," chuckles the corporal. "Private Jarmel or something—started with a *J*, anyway. I can't remember."

The two men go back to sorting mail quietly.

"Ya know, I've heard the dope in Hawaii is so potent that it makes you hallucinate. Hallucinate—wow, can you freakin' imagine, dude?"

"Really," says Teneriffe, still sorting mail.

"I'll bet every mail clerk in the world smokes weed just to get through this boring-ass shit," complains the strange corporal after a while.

"Maybe. It's funny how the recruits love their mail so much, though. I mean, when I get a letter, it feels like I just won the lottery or something. I don't care who it's from. And when they have perfume on them, forget about it."

"I know. I love that. How about SWAK?" says the strange corporal, referring to the acronym for "sealed with a kiss." Both men nod in agreement.

"Still, I wish we could smoke a big fatty right now."

Teneriffe can feel the strange corporal looking at him again. He tries to ignore the corporal and stay busy. He finishes with his big white canvas bag of mail, and then he reaches in the corner for another large white bag.

"No!" directs the strange corporal sharply. "Those are dead letters."

"Dead letters?"

"They've already been sorted. We either can't reach the addressee, or they've already been sent home," says the strange corporal.

Teneriffe is reminded of his precarious situation; he more than likely will be sent home soon, and then the letters addressed to him will be categorized as dead letters.

"Dead letters? Reminds me of the letters families get when their sons have died in combat," says Teneriffe.

"What if we could get high right now? Wouldn't that be the shit!"

This is too much for Teneriffe. He is thinking of the fallen marines who have given their lives throughout history, and this strange corporal in the mail room is trying to trick him into admitting that he smoked marijuana.

"Look, Corporal, why don't you fuck off already!" Teneriffe turns to the strange corporal with his feet apart and his head thrown back.

"Wait, what? Fuck off! Fuck you! You forget yourself, asshole!" shouts the strange corporal.

Both men are now squared off face-to-face in the small mail room with balled-up fists, about to come to blows.

"You about finished in here?" asks the staff sergeant from the adjutant's office, appearing suddenly in the portal.

"Sir, yes, sir!"

"Go back to your platoon, Tenegrief," sneers the staff sergeant.

"Sir, dismissed, aye, sir!"

THE PLATOON IS IN FORMATION at the confidence course with the other three platoons in the graduation series. The confidence course consists of fifteen or so structures laid out one after the other in an expansive green field bordered by a thick pinewood forest. The structures begin in a straight line but then arc around to the left and begin to double back toward the beginning like a giant U. The confidence course is different from the obstacle course, which is nearby in an adjacent field. The obstacle course is timed and relatively short in duration, taking only a few minutes to complete. In contrast to the obstacle course, the whole series does the confidence course, and it will take all of the afternoon to traverse. And the series will not attempt every structure. The instructors that run the confidence course will pick and choose which obstacles the series will tackle on this particular afternoon.

The first large structure that the series attempts is the infamous A frame. The A frame starts with a rope climb. After climbing the rope to the top, the marine swings a leg over a large brown log. Next, the recruit crosses a narrow rail that is high above the ground. At the end of this rail is a further climb up a two-by-six wooden lattice. Lastly, the recruit grabs an even longer rope and descends back down to the deck, lowering himself hand by hand.

"Do we have any volunteers who would like to demonstrate to the company how to traverse my A frame on this spectacular spring day?" the instructor asks in a booming voice as if he's selling used cars.

The recruits all look around and remain silent. Only the crows find this a funny joke. Just looking at the phone pole–size logs that make up this structure is enough to make the recruits' legs go wobbly.

"Oh, come on! None of you pussies want to show us how it's done?"

"I'll do it!" says Captain Jones, stepping from behind the series, much to the relief of the recruits in formation.

"Oh, very good," says the drill instructor. "You pogues are in for a real treat. Captain, don't hurt yourself now."

The captain confidently strides up to the ropes at the start of the A frame and gives the strange DI a funny smirk.

The marines are taught how to climb ropes from early in their basic training, because for many recruits, climbing a rope is a tremendous test of strength and endurance. There is actually a class devoted to teaching the recruits the proper way, and since the first time the company went to the obstacle course, they have been climbing ropes. The recruits are taught to jump up and grab the rope with both hands, wrapping one leg with the rope and then clamping the rope between their boots, creating a brake. The marines pull their legs up and clamp the rope with their boots again. Then they straighten their legs and finally reestablish their grip on the rope. As long as the brake is secure on the rope, the marines' arms are not under much strain, and it is actually pretty simple to climb a rope using lower-body strength.

Captain Jones, however, in an impressive display of upper-body strength (the captain's arms are heavily muscled and kind of Popeye-like except without any tattoos), grabs two of the ropes parallel to each other, one in either hand, and climbs up by alternating his grip on each rope. When the captain nears the top, he releases one of the ropes, grabbing the other with both hands. The captain then swings his leg over the rail and mounts the small wooden platform. Next, he quickly runs across the narrow beam. Then he jumps up the lattice in what has to be some sort of record time. Finally, the captain shimmies down the giant rope at the end of the obstacle.

"Very nice, Captain, sir! Very well done! Of course, you ladies may choose to use a single rope to climb my A frame! And don't forget to use your brake when climbing! When you get on the other side, stop and form up again as platoons before we decide how we're going to take down the rest of the confidence course today. Okay, ready! First two, go!"

All the marines in the series begin to assault the A frame in pairs.

After the whole series completes the A frame and has assembled together on the back side of the structure, the group of drill instructors running the confidence course decides to break up the series to complete the rest of the challenges as individual platoons. For the rest of the afternoon, the platoons crisscross each other, alternating on the different structures in a very organized chaos.

The fifth obstacle in order is called the slide for life, and it is the third that Teneriffe's platoon will attempt this afternoon. The slide for life offers the greatest challenge besides the A frame to many of the recruits. The marines climb up the structure using the two-by-six wooden planks that are hammered to upright poles and spaced a few feet apart. To reach the platform at the top, the recruits climb to a height of about forty-five feet. At the top, the recruits stand on the plywood platform awaiting their chance to slide down one of three large ropes attached to the top of the pole and anchored to shorter logs about seven feet above the ground. Under the rope slide is a low country pond filled with black water. The recruits get on the rope headfirst, lying with their bellies on top of the rope with one leg dangling and one leg bent so that the bootlaces are in contact and over the rope behind them. The recruits slowly inch down the rope by pulling hand over hand until they reach the other side of the pond and terra firma. Two recruits are on the rope at any one time, and there are three ropes side by side separated by about five yards. When the first recruit nears the middle, the instructors tell the next recruit to mount the rope and get started.

Teneriffe climbs to the top of the platform and stands in line with a few other recruits waiting to be told to mount the top of the ropes. He is just in time to see that Hay Fly is about a third of the way down the rope slide, flipped over and hanging upside down by his hands and his two boots crossed over the rope. Hay Fly yells out to the instructor on the ground that he cannot go on any further.

"Let go then, dipshit!" yells the instructor. "But first you better yell one out for the Marine Corps, since you're gonna get us all killed!"

Hay Fly yells out, "Oo rah! Marine Corps!" He lets go of the rope and drops like a stone into the swamp water below.

"Where you goin' now, dipshit?" yells the instructor as Hay Fly tries to hoist himself out of the black water.

Hay Fly snaps to attention, soaking wet, and yells, "Recruit Hay Fly requests permission to get out of the pond, sir!"

"First let's hear the 'Marines' Hymn,' and don't hurt our ears with any bad singing, Recruit!"

Hay Fly begins to sing the 'Marines' Hymn.' All the action comes to a complete stop on the slide for life. Everyone is silent and watching Hay Fly waist deep in water and singing. Not even the recruits on the ropes are moving. They stay still, dangling one leg pointed to the ground and the other leg behind them in contact with the rope. Some of the recruits are frozen in place many feet above the earth. Hay Fly's voice sounds proud and strong, with a surprisingly deep and melodic quality, as if he has been waiting all along for a chance to sing the 'Marines' Hymn' to everyone.

Hay Fly finishes the first verse and starts singing the second verse, which most new recruits don't know. "Oh, very nice. Continue," says the instructor.

Hay Fly finishes the second verse and starts into the third verse, which most real marines don't know. "Yes! Yes!" shouts the instructor. "Excellent, excellent!"

The whole wood, the whole battalion, has stopped, and everything is frozen for some moments.

"All right, all right, very nice. Now get the hell out of my pond, idiot! Let's go, you fish. I doubt any of the rest of you can sing that well, so stay the freak out of the drink!"

The action and commotion rises again on the slide for life. Teneriffe is instructed to start on his rope. He climbs onto the rope, placing it in the center of his chest.

Let's see; this isn't that bad. It's going to really rock when the other recruit jumps off, I bet. Teneriffe moves at a good pace with balance. *Uh oh, here comes.* Teneriffe holds on to the rope as tight as he can and stops moving, trying to cave his chest around the rope. The recruit at the far end slides over, using just his hands to hold the rope and letting his feet dangle, which causes the rope to swing and bounce.

Oh, oh, oh Lord! Hold on!

The recruit lets go and finds the ground. Now the rope really swings and bounces.

Okay, okay. I'm okay.

The rope stops bouncing and swinging. Teneriffe continues to move down the line, pulling the rope one hand over the other until he is almost to the wood post on the far side of the pond.

I did it. Not bad. Thank you, God.

Teneriffe flips over, holding on only with his hands and with his body vertical to the ground. *Whoa!*

Teneriffe lets go of the rope. He drops back down to the earth expecting to find solid ground under his feet. One foot lands on the ground, but his other foot hits the black water with a splash. Teneriffe pulls his boot out almost before it hits the sandy ground beneath the water.

Oh, crap! He tears off in a dead sprint to the next set of obstacles, which is a series of monkey bars.

"Oh, freakin' great! Wait a second! Hold on, hold on, Private! Where the freak are you going?" shouts the strange drill instructor on the ground beside the pond.

Teneriffe stops from his dead sprint to the next obstacle and then turns and shouts at attention, "Sir, this recruit is going to the next obstacle, Gunnery Sergeant!"

"Oh hell no, you're not. You just killed us all, dipshit! Now jump back in, dummy!"

"Sir, jump in, aye, sir," says Teneriffe, unable to hide his disappointment at not successfully completing the slide for life obstacle.

"Oo rah! Marine Corps!" *Better make a good splash; maybe I'll get the gunny wet!* Teneriffe does a cannonball. He surfaces, soaking wet, and whips his head like he has hair to get out of his face.

"Sir, Private Teneriffe requests permission to get out of the water, sir!"

"First recite the rifleman's creed, smart-ass!"

"This is my rifle. There are many like it, but this one is mine. It is my life. I must master it as I master my life. My rifle is my best friend. My rifle, without me, is useless. Without my rifle, I am useless. I must fire my rifle true. I must shoot straighter than my enemy, who is trying to kill me. I must shoot him before he shoots me. I will. My rifle and myself know that what counts in war is not the rounds we fire, the noise of our burst, or the smoke we make …"

"Okay, okay. Enough, dummy. Get out of the drink! What kind of platoon is this? Bunch of idiot savants or something."

"Sir, get out of the drink, aye, sir," repeats Teneriffe as he sloshes out of the pond and races for the monkey bars soaking wet.

Finally, late in the afternoon, the platoon realizes that they are the last platoon still out on the confidence course. All the other platoons have long since marched away to evening chow.

The last structure that the exhausted and stressed platoon attempts is the tower of power. Looking up at this one, Teneriffe wonders what homicidal maniac devised it. The tower is a rickety assemblage of wooden planks in four levels, and the top story is very high above the ground. None of the platforms has any sort of safety rail.

"Okay, Marines," says the strange drill instructor. "At my tower of power, you will work as a team. Because the last level is higher than you can reach on your own, you must lift each other and pull each other up if you are to reach the upper level. Marines, take your time on this one and make sure of your grip. I'm not even sure if we should have you do this one, but Gunny Morehouse assures me you pussies won't freakin' die on me or get yourselves killed. So anyway, this is the last and most difficult of the obstacles. We only lose from about five to ten percent of recruits on this structure a year, so no worries. Now let's go! Oo rah!"

"Oo rah!" shouts back the platoon.

The guide is the first to reach the top of the tower of power by having Teneriffe and the Second Squad leader lift him by the soles of his boots on the edge of the structure until he can grasp the upper story. The guide, holding on for dear, sweet life with his hands and chin, pulls himself up by swinging a leg onto the platform. After rolling around on top, the guide stands with his legs apart, hands on hips, and with an air of proud accomplishment, he views the surrounding landscape from high above the patchy green grass and brown earth.

"How does that feel, Guide?" yells up the strange drill instructor. "What's the view like up there?"

"Oo rah!" shouts the guide. "Sir, it's freakin' awesome, sir!"

"Well, let's see if the rest of you scabs can make it up there."

The guide grabs Teneriffe's arms until he can grasp the wooden plank on the edge of the platform himself. The other squad leaders lift him from his boots until, holding on with his hands and chin, he is able to swing a leg over on top of the planks. Then Teneriffe is able to roll onto the top level and stand up too. After that, the guide and Teneriffe pull up the rest of their platoon by the arms one after the other. Eventually, the whole platoon, rotating on and off the structure, has achieved the top of the tower. Only the guide and Teneriffe, the First Squad leader, stay on the top to help the others up. At last the two top recruits climb back down off the structure and fall back into formation.

The platoon begins the march back to the barracks on the way to the chow hall as the late-afternoon sun fades low on the horizon, casting orange beams that gambol across the heavens. The shadows stretch away from the marching platoon and the tall pines along the road. The recruits are exhilarated after finishing the confidence course without death or serious bodily injury and start the pretty significant march back home while listening to the song of the drill instructors.

The drill instructors sometimes sing the cadence that the platoon marches to. The singing is deep and resonant and special to the young men. It often signifies that the drill instructors are pleased with the platoon.

After a while of marching, Gunnery Sergeant Morehouse yells to Staff Sergeant Carpenter to send a runner to make sure they keep the "freakin' Gawd damn chow hall open! Tell 'em our idiots all just did the tower of power and we're coming to freakin' eat, and we're freakin' hungry!"

Boy, the confidence course! That was aptly named! What, no bungee jumping? Last platoon in, we are the studs of this series! I'm starving!

Staff Sergeant Carpenter bellows, "Agdal, come over here."

A tall, wiry recruit comes running around the platoon, and the giant Staff Sergeant Carpenter wraps his arm around Private Agdal, with his granite fist resting on Agdal's shoulder.

"Run like the very wind itself, boy, and tell them we still hasn't had no chow! Tell 'em not to dare shut down the chow line yet. We're a bunch of hungry sumbitches. Got it? Now go!"

Agdal tears off at a breakneck speed toward the Third Battalion mess hall. Staff Sergeant Carpenter turns his attention now to another matter at hand.

"Now, Tenegrief! Daggum First Squad leader got us all killed back there on the slide for life! Nice work, Tenegrief! We can't have no squad leaders getting everyone freakin' killed on no gull darn slide for freakin' life! Everyone say, 'Thank you, Private Tenegrief, for getting us all killed and making us late for chow!'"

The platoon responds, "Thank you, Private Tenegrief, for getting us all killed and making us late for chow!"

Freakin' great! Ha, making everyone late for chow. Now I know how Hay Fly feels.

"Schultz, you're First Squad leader now. We'll see how long it takes for you to screw up," says Staff Sergeant Carpenter.

It is not unusual for squad leaders to lose their position. Many recruits have been given the mantle, some for a few weeks, some for a few days, and still others for a few minutes. Teneriffe, though, has held the leadership of First Squad almost since the beginning of recruit training, and this seems a bit more solemn in its weight.

"Tenegrief, get in the freakin' back of my formation!"

"Get in the freakin' back, dummy!" piles on Sergeant Roebuck.

"Sir, get in the back, aye, sir!"

"DO YOU KNOW WHAT HAPPENS to dirtbags in the fleet that smoke weed?" Lieutenant Wolf hollers only inches from the side of Teneriffe's face.

"Sir, no, sir!" says Teneriffe at attention.

Teneriffe is back in the company commander's office, only this time he is the one standing in front of Captain Jones and Lieutenant Wolf.

"And I'm not talking about a whole freakin' baggy either, Recruit. We're talking about one frickin' little joint. Well, they get sent to Leavenworth for ten freakin' years!"

"Lieutenant Wolf is right, Recruit Teneriffe," adds Captain Jones, sitting behind his gray and silver desk. "See, it's not like the outside world. Hell, nowadays you have a bag of weed out there in the civilian world, they slap you on the wrist, maybe. But in the Marine Corps, there is zero tolerance, Recruit, and we have much more severe sentencing. Much more severe. You see what we're getting at, right? You're not entirely retarded? Are you? You understand?"

"Yeah, ya see, douchebag? Ya see?" Spittle flies from Lieutenant Wolf's mouth.

A work party of five other recruits is cleaning the office too. Only these recruits are not cleaning anything. These recruits from another platoon have instead completely stopped and are standing around watching the show. One of the cleaning party is even sitting his ass on a long green desk that was previously going unused by any living human being but is in fact home to stacks and stacks of papers.

"And at Leavenworth there's no early release! You do the whole freakin' dime! Sucker! It's not like in the civilian courts where you get sentenced to ten years and you serve six months!"

"All we're trying to say, Private, is that perhaps this isn't the best place for you right now," says Captain Jones. "We know you're a freakin' liar. You have to be. We get it! Your back is against the wall, and there is no way out. You signed and swore to one thing, and then you did the total opposite. And now you don't know what the fuck to say! Right? Am I right? We're giving you this way out, though, Private. You just have to tell the truth. That's all you have to do here."

"The truth will set you free! You freakin' ignoramus!" shouts Lieutenant Wolf

"Look, we know you're a regular user. We know—believe me, son, we know. And hey, in another world, who cares? But in my Marine Corps, we can't have people like you making his own rules and such. So for your sake, for the Marine Corps's sake, and for God's sake, tell us the truth," says the captain.

"That's right, Recruit; we know all about you. You could be home in a week, smokin' it up, sleeping in, going to movies, and jerkin' your gherkin. All you have to do now is just utter the freakin' truth for once in your pathetic life," says Lieutenant Wolf, pantomiming masturbation. "Tell us the freakin' truth, jerk-off!"

Teneriffe breaks bearing and turns his head to the right. He looks into the eyes of a light green recruit with red stubble covering his bald head. "What are you looking at?" says Teneriffe, ready to fight.

"I'm freakin' lookin' at you, fella!" says the red recruit.

"Tenegrief!" blares Lieutenant Wolf.

Teneriffe snaps his head back straight, gaze stuck to a spot on the green glass windows above the captain's head.

"Tell the freaking truth!" Lieutenant Wolf thunders.

"Recruit, now listen, I'm gonna ask you a question, and your answer is going to be of great importance to your future. Did you smoke or ingest Marijuana after your drug waiver, before you came here?" the captain asks. "Now, before you answer, Recruit, real quick, if you say you didn't and we find out later that you absolutely did smoke grass and that you're lying, well, you're going to be in some real big trouble, and I mean it, and my hands will be tied. And you'll probably be looking at some real jail time. Like maybe a few years in Leavenworth. So! Now, did you smoke or otherwise take marijuana any time before you came here to Parris Island and Marine Corps recruit training?"

"Sir, no, sir!"

There is a ringing silence in the small company office, as if all the air has been sucked out into the cement courtyard and the men are stuck in a vacuum.

"He's a fawkin' liar," a recruit says from behind Teneriffe, and then he lifts one leg up in the air and makes a farting sound with his mouth.

"This is really frustrating," laughs the captain. "Let's see what your DIs say about you." Captain Jones opens a brown folder with black lettering and an official black seal. "Recruit Teneriffe displays discipline and leadership potential, but Recruit Teneriffe likes to be liked too much by his peers to be an effective leader."

Teneriffe hears laughter all around him.

"Do you think that is an accurate assessment, Teneriffe?"

"Sir, this recruit believes in his drill instructors, sir."

"Really, well what did Gunny Morehouse tell you to tell the battalion adjutant, then? Did he say to go down to battalion there and lie your freakin' ass off?" Lieutenant Wolf mocks. "No, he freakin' didn't, did he? You maggot mother freaker!"

Teneriffe thinks two thoughts together at once, as he has noticed he can do when being challenged by a superior officer, whether on guard duty or during an inspection. As he says, "Sir, Senior Drill Instructor Gunnery Sergeant Morehouse told us to tell the battalion adjutant the truth, sir," he also thinks to himself that the gunny told his platoon that *the man* is not interested in what is best for you at all but is *really* looking out for his own career and just wants to put a feather in his own hat.

"That was a lawful freakin' order from a superior freakin' officer, you freakin' dirtbag!" Lieutenant Wolf pounds the top of the grey and green conference table in the middle of the room with his fist.

"Do you know what happens to men that smoke pot?" asks Captain Jones. "I would bet money on it that you do not. It's not pretty. Go ahead and tell him, Lieutenant Wolf. Tell the private here what happens to boys that smoke marijuana."

"They grow tits like women. Yeah, they grow big-ass floppy tits like a woman. They call them bitch tits!" says the lieutenant, straightening up with a big, sarcastic smile.

The recruits in the work party snicker.

"You actually become impotent and grow tits like a woman. Bitch tits! *Bitch tits!*" thunders Lieutenant Wolf, drawing out the words for comical effect and causing spit to sprinkle the side of Teneriffe's face. "And if you don't know what impotent means, jerk-off, let me put it this way. Your sperms will die, and you'll become, for all practical purposes, a woman. Hey, Cap'n, I think Recruit Tenegrief has already smoked so much weed that he already lies like a woman. Only men can buck up and tell the truth the way your four other pothead buddies did. You already lie like a woman! Are you a freakin' woman? Recruit? Huh? Are you? Huh? Tenegrief? Huh? Are you?"

"He's a freakin' bitch," Teneriffe hears another recruit behind him joke.

"Sir, no, sir!"

Again there is a ringing silence in the company commander's office.

Lieutenant Wolf chuckles a bit and rubs his flattop. "Agh! It's so frustrating!"

"Okay," says Captain Jones. "I'll tell you what's gonna happen, Tenegrief. We are probably going to set up an appointment for you to see the base drug exemption officer. He may have you produce another urine sample for testing, or if you are really lucky, they will do a spinal tap to remove any and all doubt that you smoked marijuana recently."

"Ya know what a spinal tap is, dick cheese? It's supposed to be the most painful thing a person can possibly experience, and it will tell definitively that you smoked marijuana," says Lieutenant Wolf.

The captain says, "Then he will definitely explain to you how we are scientifically certain that you are lying without a shadow of a doubt. And then you're going to be in a lot of trouble, Teneriffe, and there will be nothing I can do for you. By then it will be in the hands of the regimental commander, who will more than likely make his recommendation for discharge and probably jail time for wasting his valuable time. So you see, Recruit, this is going to drag on for weeks, and you probably won't see the commander for a long time, perhaps just before graduation, because he is very busy and really doesn't have time to waste on a lying sack of shit like you, Tenegrief! That's right! And this will have all been for nothing. So why don't you save yourself the torture of going all the way to graduation only to be sent home—or worse yet, jail! This is your last chance! This is it! This is the moment to save yourself a lot of pain and disgrace," says Captain

Jones solemnly. "Did you smoke or ingest marijuana before coming to recruit training depot?"

"Sir, no, sir!"

The other recruits in the office make disapproving noises.

"Oh come on."

"What a liar."

"Pussy."

"Fine," says Captain Jones. "Some people have to do things the hard way. Fine, okay. We'll just drag this thing out as long as you want, Private. I just want you to know you're not gonna make it. I suppose you're just a glutton for punishment. You like it. Well, I can promise you this: it will not be pleasant. Okay, buddy, go back to your platoon. Dismissed, Tenegrief!"

"Dismissed, aye, sir!"

I'll send the feather from my Hat!
—Emily Dickinson

"OH, FOR HEAVEN'S SAKE, SENIOR Drill Instructor Gunnery Sergeant Morehouse, look what your First Squad leader went and did to himself," says Staff Sergeant Carpenter. "Oh my Gawd!"

Staff Sergeant Carpenter is holding a towel soaked with blood to the neck of Private Schultz, who is looking tense and frustrated. Staff Sergeant Carpenter and Gunnery Sergeant Morehouse are assessing the situation in the passageway between the head and the drill instructors' office adjacent to the quarterdeck.

"What the freak happened?" sneers Gunnery Sergeant Morehouse, completely disgusted. "It looks like you shot the mother freaker in the head, Staff Sergeant Carpenter!"

"The corporal of the guard here, the incredible Private Schultz, cut himself shaving before leading this guard detail to the parade ground for that special inspection for the officer of the day," says Staff Sergeant Carpenter.

"What freakin' special inspection for the officer of the day?" spits Gunnery Sergeant Morehouse.

"You remember—the thing about the lieutenant from the IG's staff is OOD, so he wants to question a guard detail from every platoon with only a corporal of the guard and no DIs anywhere near," explains Staff Sergeant Carpenter.

Around the staff sergeant are six other privates and Private Schultz, all dressed in battle gear and mustered nearby on the quarterdeck.

"What? They were freakin' serious about that shit?" says Gunnery Sergeant Morehouse.

"Affirmative, Gunny. HQ sent a runner a few hours ago. Schultz and his whole guard detail have been practicing knowledge and cleaning their rifles and getting their uniforms ready for a few hours now. Then Schultz here wants to go cut his freakin' face off fifteen minutes until inspection. Good Christ! What the freak are we going to do now?" screams Staff Sergeant Carpenter.

"Where's the freakin' guide? He should be on this freakin' super squad thing anyway!" Gunnery Sergeant Morehouse yells. "House Mouse, where is the freakin' guide?"

"The guide is on a work detail at the NCO school, and he won't be back till around eighteen hundred hours," says the house mouse, Private Brandenburg, from a little desk on the quarterdeck in front of the DI's office without looking up.

The house mouse is another position that one of the recruits occupies for the platoon. This position is a sort of secretarial job assisting the drill instructors in various clerical duties. In this case, the house mouse is keeping track of where the various work details are and when they are expected back. Interestingly, the house mouse is usually a shorter, smaller recruit, thus making the name of house mouse physically descriptive and in line with the Marine Corps drill instructors' unusual sense of humor.

"Just freakin' great!" yells Gunnery Sergeant Morehouse. "Is this for points, Staff Sergeant? Oh, I know it is—no doubt about it. This is for freakin' points. Let's see it, Staff Sergeant Carpenter; let's see if it's stopped bleeding. Good Christ! Cover it back up! What in the freak are we gonna do now?"

Private Schultz looks intense and saddened almost to the point of tears.

Just then, Teneriffe walks through the interior stairwell, having just been questioned in the company commander's office for some time by Captain Jones and Lieutenant Wolf. Teneriffe walks straight up to Gunnery Sergeant Morehouse and says at attention, "Sir, Private Teneriffe reporting back to the platoon as ordered, sir!"

"So you're still alive, eh?" Gunnery Sergeant Morehouse sneers through his teeth.

"Sir, yes, sir!" yawps Teneriffe.

"Hey, Gunny, maybe we could put problem child Tenegrief on the special guard detail," says Staff Sergeant Carpenter. "We'll stick him in the back and maybe nobody will notice."

After some thought, Gunnery Sergeant Morehouse decides he has no other choice. "Well that's it, then. Tenegrief will have to fill in for Schultz. Schultz, go get out of your gear. You're out. Tenegrief, grab your rifle, your war belt, your gas mask, and your Kevlar helmet. You're going to be one of the special guard detail. Now move!"

The Gunny realizes that with Schultz out he will have to pick another corporal of the guard to lead the detail for the inspection at the battalion headquarters.

"Okay, now let's see … who's it going to be?" says the gunny, looking around at the other recruits of the special guard detail. "Third Squad Leader, you'll have to be the corporal of the guard. What? What it is it, son? You look pale. You're not going to pass out on me, are you, son? Look at me, Recruit. Say something!"

Teneriffe comes running up with his gear on. The house mouse helps blouse Teneriffe's top neatly as Teneriffe secures his war belt with canteens, medical kit, and ammo clips. Teneriffe also wears his gas mask fastened around his hip and roped around his granite thigh, and he wears his Kevlar helmet with elastic band stretched around the shell.

"What is it? Can't you do it?" screams the gunnery sergeant at the Third Squad leader.

"Sir, he can't do it, sir," says the house mouse, shaking his head, without looking up.

The other recruits standing around appear to share the house mouse's feeling; none of them wish to take on the mantle of leading the detail for the special inspection.

"Who can do it?" Gunnery Sergeant Morehouse demands. "Who's it going to be?"

The gunny looks around at the guard detail and Staff Sergeant Fowler, disgusted.

Slowly, the guard detail all look at Teneriffe. There is a moment of silence in which time seems suspended. Gunnery Sergeant Morehouse and Staff Sergeant Carpenter could not look more disgusted. Staff Sergeant Carpenter's hands are on his hips, and his top lip is hitched up, exposing his top row of teeth.

"Sir, I'll do it, sir," says Teneriffe.

The gunnery sergeant shakes his head from side to side and rolls his eyes up toward the ceiling. After a few moments of deep thought about what course to pursue, he says, "Okay, Tenegrief, you're gonna march this detail over to battalion." The gunny throws his hands in the air as if to say, "Why me?" "I guess it's supposed to be somewhere near the main entrance. Form up outside near the entrance, and somebody will come out for you or something. Christ! Who the freak knows! This is completely new to us too, so I'm not sure what the hell's gonna happen. They will most likely test you on your knowledge from the green monster, especially about guard duty and all that we've covered in classes. Men, look, just be cool, and everything's going to be all right. Got it? Tenegrief, march 'em over there, and all of you, for Christ's sake almighty, show some freakin' discipline!"

"Sir, aye, sir!" says Teneriffe. "Detail, fall out into the courtyard!"

The six recruits and Teneriffe double-time down the three flights of stairs and fall out into the cement courtyard.

"Fall in!" says Teneriffe.

The six recruits line up in a straight line, all facing Teneriffe. Already, the sand fleas are biting the recruits on their ears, necks, and arms.

"Look, when we get across the parade ground to battalion, we have to assume we are being watched and tested the whole time, so no fidgeting, no extra movement, and no freakin' talking. Just stand there like freakin' marines, and try to go over your knowledge in your head. I'm serious! No bullshitting around," says Teneriffe. "I don't care how long it takes for them to come out. Jus' show some freakin' discipline. And also you need to bend your legs from time to time so you don't pass out like Hay Fly did the other day in formation."

"Ten, these freakin' sand fleas are already killin' me," whines Private Collier.

"Collier, I don't freakin' care! For the next hour or so, you can't feel their little asses! Got it, Marines? Really now," says Teneriffe, "we've been here long enough to fight off the little sand bastards!" Teneriffe barks, "Uh-ten-huh! Right face. Forward march. Your left, your left, your left, right, left. Your left …"

The detail marches across the hot and wet black asphalt parade ground for the several hundred meters to reach the battalion headquarters. For some reason, perhaps the recent unexpected afternoon rain shower, the sand fleas are more plentiful and more aggressive today than ever before.

"Okay, were getting close," says Teneriffe, marching alongside the column of recruits. "When we get about twenty-five yards from the door, I'm going to call a column left march. Just the first man is going to do a left face, then the next man steps up and does a left face, and so on. Got it?"

"We all turn at once?" asks Private Fallon.

"Damn," a few of the other recruits say together.

"No! Don't all turn at once. Good question, Fallon. No, you're gonna keep marching straight until Deleón turns left, and then you take one more step and then turn left, and then we're just marching. Right, fellas?" Teneriffe says in an easy manner.

"Got it," says Private Fallon, cutting Teneriffe a funny solute with his left hand and sticking his tongue out to the side.

"Now here goes. Column, left march!"

The first recruit makes a left turn and marches parallel to the front of the building, and then the next recruit steps up and turns left and marches after. The entire special guard detail executes the maneuver well.

"Detail, halt." The men's unified movements make a stomping sound and a bang.

"Port arms!" The marines go from right shoulder arms to port arms, holding their rifles in front of their bodies. "Right face! Order arms!" The men lower their weapons to their sides. Teneriffe takes a place alongside the recruit first in line closest to the battalion's main doors.

Teneriffe says in a speaking voice, "We're gonna stand at attention for about ten minutes, Marines. Don't move until I tell you at ease. Do not break bearing to swat at sand fleas. Sand fleas got to eat same as you and me." As he says this last line, Teneriffe mimics the sound of Sergeant Roebuck's froggy drill-instructor voice.

The detail stands at attention in the steamy late-afternoon humidity planted in front of Third Battalion headquarters. The sand fleas are merciless, but the guard detail doesn't move. The sun is still high in the sky but beginning to descend to the west. The shadows slant along the redbrick facade. Cicadas chirp electric, maddening cries.

Don't these people have families? Don't they freakin' ever go home? I suppose not at Third Battalion, Recruit Training Depot, Parris Island, South Carolina.

"Ten, these things are killing me," says Private Collier.

"Don't break bearing, Marine," demands Teneriffe.

A small murder of crows, three of the large black birds, lands on the roof of the battalion building headquarters. The building's roof is low, so the large black birds are very close to the special guard detail.

"Recruit Bubba requests permission to scratch his ass, man!"

"Stand fast, Marine. Don't break bearing. We can scratch in seven more minutes."

"Caw, caw, caw!" croaks one of the crows perched atop the building.

I swear those birds freakin' laugh at us dumb-ass recruits.

"Caw, caw, caw!" responds another of the crows in agreement. The buzzing sound of the sand fleas joins in, mocking the recruits from inside their own ear canals. The rhythmic cadence of the cicadas completes the derisive cacophony.

Oh, this is pleasant. If I was this officer of the day, I would keep us out here all night long. They could get three drill instructors to yell at each one of us simultaneously. The first thing

I would do is have us perform the Marine Corps daily seven in full battle attire. We should put on our gas masks first.

"Caw! Caw! Caw!" a crow croaks again. The sand fleas buzz, and the cicadas chirp.

"I'm gonna do it, man. I'm gonna scratch," says Bubba.

"You'd freakin' better not, *esé*," says Private Deleón through clenched teeth.

"Freakin' hold it down," says Private Pierrepont. "I was just running through a field of sunflowers and roses and other beautiful shit and naked Madonna was there running toward me with love in her eyes and flowers in her hair, and you just goofed it all up."

"Madonna's a stone cold fox," says Private Fallon.

"Shut up, Fallon," says Private Pierrepont.

"Make me," laughs Private Fallon.

"Caw! Caw! Caw!"

"I'm gonna take one of these sand fleas out of my ear and squish it between my thumb and finger and kill it to death. But I'm not going to stop there. Next, I'm going to pull its tiny little wings off and then its legs and then its nose and then its hundred eyes," says Private Brickell.

"*Vamanos,* you guys! Shut the hell up!" Deleón's break from his completely stoic and almost entirely silent demeanor quiets the suffering guard detail.

Once upon a midnight dreary, while I pondered, weak and weary, over many a quaint and curious volume of forgotten lore...

"Caw! Caw! Caw!"

Nevermore

"All right, you guys," says Teneriffe after about ten minutes. "I'm going to change us to parade rest."

"It's about time, ass-munching fucktard," says Private Brickell.

"When I do, you've got two seconds to scratch before you get to parade rest," says Teneriffe, ignoring that last comment. "And if you drop your weapon, well, just keep on droppin' with it. Okay, here goes. Parade rest!"

The guard detail all start swatting the sand fleas furiously with one hand from their ears, necks, arms, and faces before eventually snapping still with legs apart, left arms behind their backs, right hands extended holding their rifle muzzles, and the butts of their rifles resting on the ground.

About ten seconds after this change, the doors of the battalion command building swing open with a crash, and three marine lieutenants and a staff sergeant come striding out the double doors.

With the crash of the doors opening, the cicadas seem to grow more exited and scream out their electric cries even louder.

"Detail, uh-ten-huh!" commands Teneriffe.

The recruits snap back to attention with heels together, left arms at their side, thumbs along the seams of their trousers, and rifles again along the right sides of their legs with the rifle butts resting on the ground. The two seconds of scratching at the sand fleas has done little to discourage the little monsters, and they again assault the guard detail's ears, necks, arms, and faces.

"Okay, let's see what we got here," says one of the lieutenants. The four men walk around the guard detail, looking over the marines. They all gather around the man on the end farthest from Teneriffe.

"Oh my God," says one of the officers. "Look at 'em all! I guess you guys never heard of Skin So Soft."

The lieutenants and the staff sergeant laugh. Avon's Skin So Soft is a lotion that marines use as an insect repellent to ward off the sand fleas. The product's name seems a bit at odds with their reputation as hard-charging leathernecks.

"Wow, they are pretty merciless today," says one of the lieutenants.

"You know how you get rid of the sand fleas, Lieutenants?" asks the staff sergeant.

"No," says one of the lieutenants. "How is that?"

"You cut a little hole in the crotch of your trousers," says the staff sergeant.

The lieutenants laugh.

One of lieutenant positions himself in front of the last recruit while the other men stand back and watch. The recruit does inspection arms, which is a complicated movement that involves lifting the rifle off the ground with the right hand and then shifting the muzzle to the left hand. Then the marine pulls back the rifle bolt with the right hand while cocking his head to the side in order to check the chamber for a round with the weapon above his head. The marine then ends with the rifle at port arms in front of the body. The inspecting lieutenant snatches the weapon from out of the hands of the marine. The marine is expected to release the rifle just as the inspecting officer snatches it. Then the marine snaps his arms to his side again, remaining at attention.

The lieutenant begins questioning Private Pierrepont on his Marine Corps knowledge while inspecting his weapon. The inspecting lieutenant and the others in the officer of the day's inspection team work their way down the row of recruits. Each recruit on the super squad does an inspection arms when the OOD squares off in front of him, and each time, the recruit surrenders his weapon and answers questions of Marine Corps knowledge.

At the third recruit, they stop and laugh as the lieutenant and the staff sergeant get really close to Private Deleón's ears. "Oh my God! Look at all the sand fleas on this one," laughs the lieutenant. "One, two, three, four, five, six, seven, eight, nine, ten, eleven, twelve. I can't count them all, ha ha ha ha ha. How 'bout you, Staff Sergeant?"

The staff sergeant is at the other ear, counting with his finger. "One, two, three, four, five, six, seven, eight, nine, ten, eleven, twelve. No way—I can't count them all! Look! His eyes are watering. What's the matter, son? These little harmless fleas bothering you? You want to scratch? You want to scratch, don't you, son, don't you? Go ahead and scratch. It's okay!"

"Sir, no, sir!" yells Private Deleón.

"Yes, you do," says the staff sergeant. "Don't lie. Look, he's shaking all over, and his eyes are watering." Actually, all seven recruits are beginning to shake and tear up with the strain.

"It's okay to scratch," says the inspecting lieutenant, addressing the whole detail. "Go ahead and scratch, detail. I know you want to." The lieutenants stop and wait. "Go ahead, seriously, it's okay."

"Don't you want to scratch?" the staff sergeant asks.

"Sir, no, sir!" yells the guard detail in unison.

"Okay," says the lieutenant, shaking his head with some resignation.

The lieutenant begins to question the men one at a time again. Several minutes pass while the special guard detail answers questions. About a quarter of an hour later, the lieutenant finishes testing Private Brickell, and he and one lieutenant to his right do a left face, take a step, and then a right face, arriving directly in front of Teneriffe. Teneriffe performs the inspection arms maneuver. The Lieutenant snatches the black M16A2 from his hands.

Yeah, ah, I don't really like that very much at all.

The inspection arms maneuver is an act of military discipline and shows respect for the chain of command. Giving up one's weapon is a symbolic act showing fealty to a superior officer. Still, Teneriffe is entitled to feel less than pleased with having his rifle snatched from his grasp.

"Mm hmm," says the lieutenant as he inspects Teneriffe's weapon. "See, look at this," the lieutenant says to the staff sergeant. The staff sergeant steps up to the lieutenant's left shoulder.

"Yes, sir, see where the carbon will start to build up next to the magazine release lever," says the staff sergeant.

"Yes, see that carbon residue inside the chamber?" the lieutenant says, holding the black rifle in front of Teneriffe's face so he can look into the chamber.

"Sir, yes, sir!"

"You know you can use a cotton swab and CLP to get that carbon right up. Where are you from, Private?"

"Sir, I'm from Warner Robins, Georgia, sir!"

"Alabama is a wonderful state," says the lieutenant, handing Teneriffe back his weapon.

An unusual response is one of the things any soldier has to get used to during questioning. It is possible that the lieutenant is trying to be funny by implying that Georgia isn't so great of a state but its neighbor Alabama is.

"Sir, aye, sir!" Teneriffe affirms, at a loss.

"What is your seventh general order?"

"Sir, this marine's seventh general order is to talk to no one except in the line of duty, sir!"

"What is your eighth general order?"

"Sir, this marine's eighth general order is to give the alarm in case of fire or disorder, sir."

"What is your ninth general order?"

"Sir, this marine's ninth general order is to call the corporal of the guard in any case not covered by instructions, sir."

"Who is the corporal of the guard?"

"Sir, I am the corporal of the guard, sir!"

"What would you do if, when on fire watch one fateful night, someone were to sound an alarm of some sort?"

"Sir, I would … in the case of an alarm at night, I would most likely alert my drill instructors, sir."

"Really? Now how would that work in the fleet, I wonder?" slyly ponders the strange lieutenant. "They don't have drill instructors in the fleet, do they, Corporal of the Guard?" says the lieutenant, looking over his shoulder at the staff sergeant with a wry smile.

"Sir, no, sir."

"What year was the Marine Corps founded?"

"Sir, the Marine Corps was founded in 1775, sir." *These sand fleas are killing me. Stop shaking! I can't.*

"Where was it founded?"

"Sir, the birthplace of the Marine Corps is Tun Tavern, sir." *I can't believe nobody on the guard detail has swatted or scratched. I'm dyin'.*

"What city was Tun Tavern in?"

"Sir, Tun Tavern was in Philadelphia, Pennsylvania, sir." *Oh, come on! Look, even the inspectors are swatting and scratching at the sand fleas.*

"What year did World War II start?"

"Sir, the United States entered World War II in 1941, sir!" A shudder goes through Teneriffe's spine, and a tear falls down his cheek.

"Wow," says the lieutenant, taken aback. "You guys look miserable. Tell ya what I'm going to do. You marines make sure you clean those rifles well, especially in those places with the carbon buildup that I showed you. Other than that"—the lieutenant turns to the other members of his inspection party—"I'd say really your bearing and knowledge were outstanding. The best of the regiment, don't you think?"

"No doubt," laughs one of the lieutenants.

"Affirmative," says the staff sergeant.

"Okay, then," says the inspecting lieutenant. "Corporal of the Guard, march this detail back to your platoon and tell Gunny Morehouse you guys did pretty well."

"Sir, aye, sir!" Teneriffe commands, "Detail, rifle salute!" The recruits all cut a salute with their left hands down to the fluted muzzle of the M16A2s on their right legs.

The inspector's party snaps to attention and salutes. The lieutenants and the staff sergeant then go back inside the battalion headquarters. The battalion doors crash shut with a loud clang, and the murder of crows flies off, startled by the sound.

"Caw, caw, caw!"

"At ease!" says Teneriffe.

The recruits on the special guard detail let out sighs of relief. The green recruits swat and scratch at all their exposed surfaces.

ON ANOTHER SUNNY AFTERNOON LATER that week, the platoon marches to an indoor swimming pool to participate in the swim qualification section of basic warrior training. The Olympic swimming pool is located in a hangar-size building whose upper part and ceiling are Plexiglas. One side of the pool has old wooden bleachers, on which the platoon sits for classroom session. At one end of the pool is a low diving board and a high diving board. All around the pool are lifesaving rings, floating dividers, and other pool gear.

The head swimming instructor looks at the platoon of worn-out recruits. They are tired, and he knows why. The training is intentionally brutal. "During my next period of instruction, if I speak too loud, too soft, too fast, or too slow, feel free to let me know! And if you have a question, I want you to stand up! Announce your name and where you're from, and ask your stupid question! If you feel *sleepy* or *tired* during my freakin' instruction, I want you to get the freak up and stand to the side of my bleachers! That being said, if you do fall asleep in my freakin' classroom, and because this shit is life or death, I will personally kill you! Do you read me?" the head swimming instructor thunders.

"Sir, yes, sir!" shouts the platoon.

"I can't hear you!"

"Sir, yes, sir!" The noise booms off the water and the cold walls.

"There are three levels for swim qualification in my Marine Corps. The lowest level is level three, the minimum requirement to be a United States Marine. Okay, who doesn't know how to swim? Raise your hands." About fifteen of the recruits timidly raise their hands. "I don't want you to be nervous or intimidated. We are going to teach you all you need to know today to pass level three Marine Corps swim qualification. In fact, me and my fellow swimming instructors are so good at what we do, we are going to teach every single last one of you how to pass to level two!"

The head swimming instructor goes on to explain to the platoon how the swim qualification will be completed. The platoon is to be broken up into groups. The first group, comprised of the recruits that do not know how to swim, will break off and go to the shallow end of the pool to learn the basics of swimming in order to pass the level-three requirements. The other group, the majority of the platoon, will begin to tread water for forty-five minutes as the first part of the level-two qualification.

As the head swimming instructor lectures about aspects of the swim qual, another instructor demonstrates the techniques in the water. The head swim instructor first lectures the platoon on how to tread water by slowly moving the arms and legs and fanning out the water in order to maintain one's head above the surface. At the same time, another instructor actually treads water in the pool.

The head instructor also explains that part of the treading-water requirement is making a life preserver with the recruit's trousers. He says that by tying off the legs of the trousers and blowing bubbles up into the waist, it is possible to fill the trousers with air and that the trousers will act as a replacement for an actual life preserver in the water. The marine will cinch the waist tight with his belt after filling the trousers with air, and after tying the legs together, he can slip it over his head and around his neck just like a regular life vest.

The next part of the swim qual will be assisting a drowning swimmer back to the edge of the pool. One recruit acts as a swimmer in distress while the other recruit swims up behind him. By reaching with one arm around the swimmer's neck and under his armpit so as not to choke him, the rescuer can tow the other recruit on his back and swim by using his other arm. The danger, explains the head swim instructor, is that the drowning swimmer is panicking and thrashing about in the water, and there is a real possibility that he could end up drowning both men. The key element is to approach and secure the drowning swimmer from behind.

The last part of the qualification will be swimming the length of the pool using three different strokes: the breaststroke for fifty meters, the sidestroke for fifty meters, and the freestyle for fifty meters. Again, one of the other instructors demonstrates the three different strokes. Teneriffe is familiar with the breaststroke and the freestyle, but although Teneriffe has been swimming his whole life and was taught by his father, who was a competitive swimmer in college, he has never heard of the sidestroke before, and this concerns him. The sidestroke, explains the swimming instructor, is swimming on one's side and reaching out in front with a one-arm stroke while using a sideways scissor kick.

Lastly, the head swim instructor explains how a marine qualifies for the highest swim qualification, or CWS-1. One of the other swim instructors climbs up the high diving board. When he reaches the top, his legs and feet are tied together with three of the tan canvas belts that the marines wear around the waists of their trousers, and another instructor ties his hands around his back. Next, the instructor jumps into the deep end of the pool off the high diving board. The bound swimmer surfaces to breathe and continues to swim, using dolphin kicks to propel himself in the water. The head swim instructor says that he will have to continue in this fashion for at least ten minutes to attain the highest rank in the Marine Corps swim qualification.

"Most marines don't ever need to qualify CWS-1. And it's not needed to graduate from boot camp, so none of you are required to do the test at all, ever! We just wanted to show you what the test is so maybe in the future when you swim qual in the fleet you may want to try and go for it," explains the head swim instructor. "Oo rah!"

"Oo rah!" shouts the platoon.

"We may, at the end of the day, allow a few of you to try the first level if we have enough time—and if any of you are hard charging enough to go for it. Do you think any of you slimy sons of bitches can do that? I doubt it! I don't think so!"

I have to try that!

"Now let's break up into groups and get started! All my nonswimmin' pogues get to the shallow end. Everyone else stay here, and we'll begin treading water in groups."

The swim qual is fun for Teneriffe. It is an example, once again, that something in his past has given him a significant advantage over most of the other recruits. In this instance, as has been mentioned before, Teneriffe spent most of his childhood and adolescent summers swimming, playing, and hanging out for hours at the officers' club pool surrounded by family and friends. For him, the pool is not to be feared in any way; it is to be enjoyed.

Treading water for forty-five minutes is the first exercise for most of the platoon. A few of the squad leaders float together; at times, they listen to and laugh at the ones in the platoon trying to make the third level for swim qual in the shallow end.

Everyone in the platoon is wearing camouflaged trousers and green skivvy shirts with no boots or socks.

Teneriffe tries to calm some of the others who are worried about making it the whole time. "We're gonna make forty-five minutes—no problem. You can tread water for days if you have to. It's so easy."

The head swim qual instructor breaks off from the nonswimmers in the shallow end, and he strides around to see the ones treading water on the outside edge of the pool. He walks up to Teneriffe's group and says, pointing, "You guys try doing the life-preserver trick with your trousers."

Teneriffe and his group all take off their trousers while still treading water. Next, Teneriffe ties the end of his trouser legs shut with the green satin tie strings that are sown into the ends of the trousers. After that is done, Teneriffe ties the ends of the pant legs to each other. He then submerges, holding the waist of his trousers open above him and blowing air bubbles out of his mouth. He has to come up for air several times in order to inflate his trousers, and it becomes a bit of a competition among Teneriffe's small group of swimmers who can finish his modified life preserver first. Teneriffe closes the waist and ties it tight with his belt. The first couple of marines start to float on the surface with the puffed-up camouflaged trousers around their necks like life vests. The members of the small group begin to recline in the water, not having to exert any energy to stay afloat.

"Very nice! This group right here! Very nice!" says the head swim qual instructor, pointing at Teneriffe's group, so everyone in the building can hear.

When Teneriffe's group is done treading water, they sit on the bleachers, quietly reading their green monsters and watching the sadly funny prospect of men trying to learn how to swim in a single day.

During the next phase of qualifications, the marines must save a drowning victim. Teneriffe jumps in and swims around Private Peters, who is pretending to drown. Ten swims up and grasps Private Peters around his neck and arm from behind. He quickly turns and reaches for the edge of the pool with the stocky private flailing like a distressed swimmer on his back.

"Good! Very strong!" says the swim qual instructor.

For most of the platoon, the requirement to swim three different strokes is next. However, two recruits still struggling to learn basic swimming are surrounded by instructors in the shallow end of the pool.

Teneriffe and a few other recruits jump in at the deep end and begin swimming the length of the pool doing the breast stroke. Teneriffe does the breaststroke quickly.

"Very good! Very nice! What's your name, Recruit?"

"Sir, Private Teneriffe, sir!" says Teneriffe, looking up out of the pool between strokes. He reaches the end of the first fifty meters, turns around, and begins the sidestroke. Unfamiliar with this swimming stroke, Teneriffe lurches awkwardly on his side and struggles to time the kick correctly.

"Oh Lord, no! That stinks, Tenegrief! Oh good God! Get it together, Tenegrief! I thought you were a shark! Instead you're a flounder!" the head swim instructor begins to mock.

Well, hell, I've never heard of such a thing. A side stroke. Teneriffe grows angry in the water. *I think it's a bit feminine looking, to be clearly honest!*

He reaches the wall at the end of the pool and flips to turn, pushing off the wall hard, and comes up for the last fifty meters in the freestyle swim. Teneriffe kicks furiously, churning a wake behind him and lifting his body halfway out of the water, displaying thews of steel. He hits the wall, and the wake comes crashing up behind him. Teneriffe jumps up out of the pool, pushing off the concrete deck with his hands.

"Hey, you! Come here!" the head swim qual instructor yells, pointing at Teneriffe and sounding angry.

Teneriffe walks quickly in soaking camouflaged trousers and drab green skivvy T-shirt to a group of three swim qual instructors hovering over a recruit in the pool. The recruit in the water is trying to complete the swimming section of the swim qual, but this poor guy is struggling mightily. He tries to do the sidestroke. His head is turned to the side, but his body is underneath him, dangling vertically in the water instead of floating horizontally. The light green marine struggles to stay afloat by clawing at the water in front of him with his arms, but he is going nowhere. He begins to hyperventilate as the pool water splashes in his mouth and nose. Right over him, hovering beside the pool, the three swim qual instructors stand with crossed arms, mocking and derisive. The swim qual instructors wear khaki recon swim trunks and blue, shiny T-shirts; calf-high white athletic socks; and blue Nike running shoes.

"Oh, this don't look good!"

"I don't think you're gonna make it there, fella!"

"Try swimming, dipshit!"

The swimmer begins to make gurgling sounds while hyperventilating: "Ah ah ah ah ..."

"Ah ah ah ha ha! What a dip wad!"

"This is freakin' pathetic!" "Sniff."

"You'd think that before joining the world's largest amphibious fighting force, you would know how to freakin' swim—duh!"

"You're not gonna make it! I don't feel like gettin' wet again today, dumbass! So that means you're freakin' gonna die, dip wad!"

The head swim qual instructor turns to Teneriffe, who stands at attention.

"Sir, Private Teneriffe reporting as ordered, sir."

"So, Tenegrief, where you from? Did you swim in high school for your school or something?"

"Sir, no, sir. I'm from Warner Robins, Georgia. We had football and spring football, sir."

"Were you a lifeguard or something?"

"Sir, no, sir."

"Well, do you want to try to go for first-class swim qual today?"

"Sir, yes, sir!"

"Well, now hold on, Tenegrief, now hold on. Let me think," says the head swim qual instructor, sounding surprised. "Get back in the pool and do the sidestroke again. Let me see that shit again, but this time take it easy, bam bam! Take it slow and under control. You barely need to kick. Remember, slow and easy."

"Sir, aye, sir," says Teneriffe. He walks quickly to where he got out of the pool. Teneriffe jumps down into the pool again, and he attempts once more to swim the sidestroke.

"No, no, no! Get the hell out! Get out! No way! You suck! No way!" yells the head swim qual instructor. "Get out!"

Teneriffe jumps out of the pool, and again he goes and sits on the wooden bleachers to dry off. Teneriffe is disappointed, but ... *The side stroke. I mean, who ever heard of such a thing? I never heard of that stuff before today.*

"Uh oh, I don't think he's gonna make it!" says one of the swim qual instructors, hovering over the submerged recruit.

"How long has he been down there for now?"

"I don't know. A while, I guess. I can still see bubbles."

"Here, hold this," the head swim qual instructor says and hands a clipboard and whistle to one of the others.

The head instructor jumps in and emerges quickly with the big green recruit, whom he hands up into the grasp of the two other swim qual instructors. The recruit lies prone on the side of the pool and spits up water, looking dazed and confused, while the head swim qual instructor jumps from the pool.

"Let him lie down over on the bleachers. Let 'im rest awhile." The head swim qual instructor laughs and says, "I guess he sank well enough to make second level." The other swim instructors all laugh.

Later, the platoon is all finally out of the pool and on the bleachers and pretty much dry. The last recruits are sitting down on the wooden bleachers when the head swim qual instructor approaches the platoon again.

"Okay! Not bad! Everybody pretty much passed swim qual today! But some of you have a lot of work to do when you get out to the fleet! I mean really! A lot of work to do! So good luck for the rest of basic training, and good luck out in the fleet if you make it there! Finally, earlier one of your fellow recruits expressed to me that he wanted to try for first-class swim qual today, CWS-1! So why the freak not! Tenegrief! Do you still want to go for it?"

"Sir, yes, sir!"

"Okay! First you have to sign this waiver that says if you die your folks and all won't sue us and shit," says the head swim qual instructor. Then he laughs and says, "Just bullshittin' ya, Private. You already signed that one a long time ago."

Teneriffe gets up, takes his boots and drab socks off again, and walks to the high dive. As Teneriffe begins to climb the metallic gray ladder, he wonders why he accepted this challenge. Adrenaline surges through his body, preparing his muscles for exertion.

What was I thinking? I could die. No, wait, I can do this. Just remain calm. I've never done anything even remotely similar to swimming with my hands and feet tied together. I thought it looked fun though. Sure it is! It will be a gas! Stay calm. You can do this. It's all about staying calm and letting your body do what it has done your whole life—play games at the pool!

Teneriffe automatically keeps reaching hand over hand on the sides of the ladder, lifting his body higher and higher. At the top, an instructor that has followed him to the top of the high diving board ties Teneriffe's hands behind his back and his feet and legs together with khaki canvas belts. Teneriffe hops to the end, takes a look at the water to judge the distance, looks at his platoon sitting on the wooden bleachers by the side of the pool and looking up at him, and takes several deep breaths, trying like hell to slow his breathing. He continues the internal self-affirmations that bolster his resolve to attain the highest swimming qualification, CWS-1, for the United States

Marines. With little hesitation, he takes one last big breath and jumps from the board.

On his way down, before drilling through the surface of the pool, he shouts loudly like the instructor did at the beginning of the swimming qualification event, "Oo rah! Marine Corps!"

Teneriffe breaks the surface of the water with his feet pointed and drills directly to the bottom of the pool. He quickly pushes off the bottom and heads for the surface, toward air and life. As he breaks the surface, he gulps the air and begins to propel himself slowly with small dolphin kicks. He decides to stay close to the surface for a time, continually raising his head out of the water for breaths. After a few minutes and with bolstered confidence, Teneriffe decides to dive deep once more for a spell. He breaches the surface this time with a large inhalation and then thrusts his head down hard and kicks his flukes up into the air. He reaches the bottom of the pool again and scours the bottom for loose change as if he were in the pool at the officers' club back home on Robins Air Force Base.

Finally, after around ten minutes of Teneriffe slowly circling the deep end of the pool and the platoon quietly reading their green monsters or watching Teneriffe swim for the highest swim classification, the head swim qual instructor exclaims to all, "He's got ten seconds!"

The platoon counts down, "Ten, nine, eight, seven, six, five, four, three, two, one!"

Teneriffe kicks to the shallow end of the pool until he can stand up. One of the other swim instructors unties his hands and legs and slaps him on the back.

"Nice job! Nice job, Tenegrief! Well done! Well done! Now get the freakin' hell outta there!" shouts the swim qual instructor.

The platoon claps and cheers as Teneriffe gets out of the pool.

14

"AT EASE, RECRUIT. HAVE A seat," says the dark green staff sergeant. "Now, I really want you to be completely at ease. Please do not think of me as a staff sergeant in the United States Marine Corps. I want you to pretend that we aren't even at Parris Island today at all."

The staff sergeant isn't even in a uniform. The floor of the small office is a shiny wooden deck that looks like it belongs aboard an old wooden ship. He sports a teal three-button cotton Izod pullover, highly starched and sharply creased khaki pants, and brown penny loafers. The staff sergeant also wears the latest round tortoiseshell eyeglasses, and his posture seems very relaxed; he reclines in his dark wooden chair with one leg crossed over the other knee.

"We're just two guys having a normal conversation about drugs and their effect on the human body. I'm going to ask you some questions, but mostly I'm going to give you some knowledge, and then afterward, I'm going to send in my recommendation to the colonel as to whether you should stay here at Parris Island and complete your basic warrior training or whether you should be shipped home. Please, I really don't want you to feel guarded or nervous. I really just need you to be honest with me and with yourself."

Staff Sergeant Benning is a ten-year veteran of the Marine Corps, and he really likes being the base drug exemption officer. He likes to help young marines get out of difficult situations involving drugs and alcohol if they truly want to turn their lives around. He feels that he can make a difference. He also believes that he is tough enough to get rid of the undesirable marines that are hopeless liars, degenerates, and con artists who seek only to destroy his beloved Marine Corps.

"Let me start by explaining a few things. My job on base is to help marines get help when they feel they have a drug- or alcohol-related problem. However, there are some conditions. See, if a marine comes to me after he or she has come up positive on a piss test, it is too late for me to help that marine. The marine has to come to me before we find out from a positive drug-screening test result. Then we can send that marine to rehab until they're all better. What do you think about that? In the civilian world, rehab can run into the tens of thousands of dollars, but in the service, it is free, which is an excellent benefit if you ever do become a marine, Teneriffe. Is that how you say it? Teneriffe?"

"Sir, my drill instructors call me *Tenegrief*, sir."

"Oh, ha! That's funny, really. Okay, Tenegrief! I'm going to say right off the bat that it doesn't look good for you here now," says the staff sergeant, shaking his head. "Listen, the piss test only shows recent and long-term continual drug use. There is no way that the test can be wrong. We are quite sure of this fact. Now, I don't know if you've been told, but there is zero tolerance for drugs in the service. It's been that way for some time now, and that's the way we like it. Those marines that pop positive on the urinalysis, well, they're discharged, usually dishonorably, and they get brig time. And the sentences are much longer than in civilian courts nowadays. My point is, Tenegrief, we are very confident in our tests. Do you have anything to say?"

Teneriffe tries to think of a response. He wants so badly to impress this man, to show this marine that he is capable and worthy. Yet at this moment, Teneriffe is at a loss, and he can think of nothing to say that wouldn't sound like a crass lie.

"No, staff sergeant."

"Well, I'm going to recommend that you be released from recruit training. I know our tests are accurate, and I believe you are not being completely truthful with me."

The staff sergeant writes on the inside of the brown folder with the black Marine Corps insignia on the outside. Teneriffe is careful not to display any physical movements. This would be a major break in his military bearing and would betray his disappointment at hearing the staff sergeant's words. He feels like dropping his head. His heart pounds in his chest, his mouth gets dry, and his palms and armpits start to sweat. Teneriffe tries to cope with the idea that the interview and his initial warrior training experience at Parris Island will soon come to a failing conclusion.

"Now," says the strange staff sergeant, "aside from being the unit's drug exemption officer, I'm currently doing drug and alcohol rehabilitation and counseling here on base. Let me tell you marijuana and its active narcotic ingredient, THC, is most assuredly a gateway drug to other harmful mood-altering, mind-altering substances. Right now, cocaine, and especially crack cocaine, is the scourge of our great land. They are literally fighting a war in the streets of our nation's urban centers fueled by the underworld narcotic trafficking of this crack cocaine. And it's in the suburbs too. It's everywhere, frankly. But ya know what? It ain't going to be here, by God! Not in my Marine Corps! Where are you from, Tenegrief?"

"Sir, I'm from Warner Robins, Georgia, sir."

"No way! I'm from Moultrie! Wow, no way, I'm just down the way in Moultrie! Damn fine football in Warner Robins," says the staff sergeant, seeming to get off track somewhat.

This cheers Teneriffe and gives him a glimmer of hope. The staff sergeant has been dour and monotone throughout the interview but now is animated and excited.

"Sir, yes, sir, but y'all beat us my junior year," says Teneriffe.

"Oh, wait! Really? Wait!" says the staff sergeant, lost in thought, holding a hand up in the air.

"Y'all were really big that year," adds Teneriffe. "The offensive line must have averaged like two sixty."

"Okay, wait—I remember that game. So wait, you're not a Demon?"

The staff sergeant is referring to the other school in Warner Robins, the one that bears the city's name. The Warner Robins Demons have won two state championships and two national championship titles in 1976 and 1981.

"No, sir. I'm an Eagle, sir," says Teneriffe, explaining that he played for the crosstown rival school, the Northside Eagles.

"Man, that was a great game, a great game. I think we only won it in the last few seconds. What a game!" The staff sergeant sounds very happy, and his whole countenance has changed. He beams a grand smile.

"Y'all had a big young freshman fullback that was a monster," says the staff sergeant. "What was his name—Tubbs?"

"Yes, sir, we did. He ran all over y'all. If it wasn't for those home cookin' refs, we might have won it," says Teneriffe.

"Oh, home cookin', bull frog! We took that one fair and square."

The staff sergeant and Teneriffe laugh together, and Teneriffe reckons that, miraculously, the relationship has changed for the better. The staff sergeant continues to write in the folder on his desk, laughing and shaking his head.

Finally, after a few minutes, the staff sergeant says, "Well, let's get back to the issue at hand. You must know Warner Robins is a big drug-trafficking hub, really all of middle Georgia. The drugs come up from Florida, and then Warner Robins is right smack dab in the center of the state, right before you get to Atlanta and the rest of the south and eastern seaboard. And cocaine is such a terrible problem now. Marijuana is bad too, but coke is the worst. You can get addicted the first time you try cocaine. The first time! It's just a scourge. It's a blight on the land. Cocaine is like a thousand orgasms. That's what they say the effects are like. A thousand orgasms. Can you imagine? It's no wonder that's all people want to do. They did a test on mice with it. The mice were given a choice between the drug and food to keep them alive, and the mice chose the coke and died! Just terrible, awful.

"And take heroin, for instance. People overdose and die from it all the time. *Sixty Minutes* did a program that claimed that most of the United States Armed Forces were high on heroin and marijuana after the Vietnam War. That is where zero tolerance began. Heroin! I mean come on, do we want our defense forces on freakin' heroin! That's not the type of volunteer army we want and demand as the greatest nation on earth. And did you know that marijuana is a schedule I drug the same as heroin and other opiates, according to our government? I really don't want my marines to be all stupid and silly on grass. Not in my by God Marine Corps!

"I'm not sure if you were aware, but marijuana will actually retard your body's ability to produce testosterone too, Tenegrief. That's right!" the staff sergeant says, nodding. "As a man, as a former football star, you want to do everything you can to increase your testosterone production, not hurt it. Professional athletes—football players, Tenegrief—actually take testosterone injections just to raise their testosterone some more. Furthermore, Marijuana will also cause psychological damage too,

Tenegrief. You'll quite literally go insane from smoking too much!"

Oh, that will never happen.

"And smoking is just stupid when you talk about human health and fitness, which marines are fanatical about. No one can score as well on the physical fitness test if they smoke as if they didn't. Smoking weed can lead to heart disease, respiratory ailments, respiratory diseases, and sterilization. Did you know that you can get enlarged breasts from smoking weed, Tenegrief?"

"Sir, yes, sir. I believe they call them bitch tits, sir."

"Yes, that's right, they are referred to as bitch tits," laughs the staff sergeant. "Ha ha ha, that's right, bitch tits."

"So there's all that evidence," says Staff Sergeant Benning. "And I know there's a lot of talk about drinking, especially here at PI. Every instructor's class begins with a good drinking story and all, but I think the Marine Corps's going to start comin' down on alcohol too. And it's going to be much more severely punished than in the past. I've already submitted a three-strikes-and-you're-out policy as far as that is concerned. The first time you screw up from drinking, you would be seen by a counselor who suggests some treatment, and the marine would have to go to mandatory Alcohol Anonymous or Narcotics Anonymous meetings and would be required to remain sober. The second incident would require a stay at rehab, and the third time would mean dishonorable discharge. And remember, Tenegrief, you won't even be able to drink legally for a couple of years, so for you, it's just as illegal as marijuana or LSD.

"I mean, Tenegrief, I see the terrible effects of all these drugs, alcohol included, every day. Otherwise productive, strong, and heroic marines succumb to these brutal addictions, and it just breaks your freakin' heart to see them used up and pitiful and usually in handcuffs. Drugs and alcohol are just a trap. That's all they are, Tenegrief. Addicts that I work with every day say that one fix is all it takes to get hooked and that a thousand times is never enough to satisfy the need.

"Well, let me hear in your own words how you think you could have come up with a positive result on your urinalysis."

"Sir, well ..." Teneriffe sits pensively, slouched over forward with his muscled forearms across his knees, looking at his shiny black combat boots. Teneriffe thinks to himself that he must say something. If he remains silent, he will surely get a bad evaluation. "Sir, in health class in high school we were taught that everyone's body is different and reacts differently to food, plants, and drugs. People have just crazy food allergies where they break out in hives all over their bodies from seafood. They have allergies from peanuts that shut their throats and suffocate them, or if one of them should get stung by a bee, they could easily die. So, like, I'm thinking that no two people are the same from a health and well-being standpoint. Perhaps that one time that I smoked marijuana eight months ago was somehow enough in my body to cause a positive result on the drug test. Like maybe my fat cells retain THC longer than other normal human beings or something."

The drug exemption officer looks at Teneriffe from his boots to the top of his head. "Hmm, perhaps, perhaps," says the drug exemption officer. "Perhaps. You do look a little puffy." The staff sergeant leans over on his desk and writes more inside the brown folder.

I look what?

The staff sergeant reclines back into the wooden rolling chair. "Okay, let me finish up this report. I have to say I'm still leaning in favor of your dismissal from Marine Corps basic training, but first I'm going to do some more research and think about our talk here today. Okay, when I dismiss you, I want you to go back to the van that you came in."

This again makes Teneriffe apprehensive. However, there is a glimmer of hope. The two of them bonded over football and are from the same area. And Teneriffe is proud of his reply when asked what could have caused a positive result on his drug screen. He knows it's false, of course, but it was not totally incoherent. Perhaps it even sounded plausible.

"Sir, the big green van, sir?"

"Yes, the gunnery sergeant that drove you here will bring you back to your platoon barracks for now."

The staff sergeant stands up and extends his hand. Teneriffe stands up and shakes the staff sergeant's hand and thanks him for the knowledge.

"Well, better luck next season, Tenegrief!"

"Oh, we'll get ya back, sir."

TENERIFFE SITS ALONE IN A large green van that seems
even bigger with only one person occupying the enclosed
bubble. It's one of those official military vans that have
like seven giant rows of white bench seats. These moments
that Teneriffe is alone are in such stark contrast to the rest
of recruit training that it makes Teneriffe smile. Just the
fact that he is in an automobile is sweet and rare.

*I can't wait to fly over the surface of the planet at a high
rate of speed.*

Teneriffe remembers the first forced march from the
receiving barracks all the way out into the woods to
third battalion. To a boy that had rarely worn hard shoes,
preferring to go barefoot most of the time with his toes
squishing in the red Georgia clay beneath the burning
Georgia sun, black combat boots were extremely painful
to get used to. That first forced march was the hardest
thing Teneriffe had to endure throughout all the trials
and tribulations of basic training. The pain in his feet and
ankles was almost overwhelming. He was only able to
complete the march by looking around and observing the

stoic demeanor of the other recruits immediately around him as they strode confidently on.

The door slams. A strange gunnery sergeant jumps into the driver's seat behind the enormous white steering wheel of the giant green government van. The engine turns over, and they are on their way.

"How did it go, Tenegrief?"

"Sir, the drug exemption officer said he's recommending me for discharge, sir!"

"No way! You know, a lot of us here are hoping you'll make it to graduation. I've been in the corps for thirteen years, and I can tell you all this drug testing is very recent. Hell, in the old corps, we all used to smoke dope like crazy. Those were the good ol' days, my friend. On a Friday night, we used to party! You could go to any room, and everyone had some. Now it's all this political bullshit. Piss tests and rehab—ha. You're probably just like me when I enlisted. You work hard and you party hard. Am I right?"

"Sir, yes, sir!"

The gunny smiles and looks in the rearview mirror. "Ah, I thought so. You probably had all the chicks too. Weed and sex is the best. I used to love it. Now we drink real hard! I have to confess, I miss the days of grass instead of booze. Alcohol … alcohol ruins lives. It's just a bunch of bullshit, outlawing a beautiful plant made by God. Marines get drunk, they get all froggy and crazy and get in trouble. It absolutely ruins their lives. Their wives leave them; they get in accidents. I'd just as soon smoke a hundred joints as look at alcohol. With alcohol, you get all fat and hungover. The day after drinking, you feel like your head's been smashed with a sledgehammer. Give me a break. Dope has none of that. Look, you can tell me, man to man, and nobody will know. And now, since you said you're going home anyway, you smoked pot, didn't you?"

"Sir, no, sir. The test results were wrong."

"Tenegrief, I just admitted to you that I smoked a hell of a lot of weed in my day. You're saying you never smoked any; come on. I know better, son."

Teneriffe wonders if the gunnery sergeant is being truthful or if this is another attempt to trick him into a confession. Maybe it is and maybe it isn't. Teneriffe decides to heed Cookie's warning to stick to his guns and confide in no one.

"Sir, that is what I'm saying, sir!"

"You're a freakin' liar," the gunnery sergeant says angrily.

"Sir, aye, sir."

The strange gunnery sergeant and Teneriffe drive in silence for some time. Teneriffe looks out the window at the manicured green lawns that go meandering by in front of the white and green buildings and the more modern redbrick ones. The van passes several recruit platoons from First, Second, Third, and Fourth Battalions. Thick green lines of boys and girls drift along the sides of the van like timber on a river.

The drill instructors sing out under their green felt Smokey Bear covers, "Low, righty, lay oh, low, righty, lay oh! Low, righty, lay oh, low, righty low!"

All along the way, drill instructors are punishing marine recruits with push-ups, or bend-and-reaches, or mountain climbers.

Look how many! Sons and daughters of America! Look at that platoon; they already have high-and-tights. Not at Third Battalion—not until after wilderness week. Wow, that platoon is really good; they must be close to graduation. I've never seen that drill move before.

Then the van drives by Fourth Battalion, the battalion that trains women marines.

Look at the chicks!

It's a white light—it's like looking at the sun reflecting off the glass—and they are gone. *They were cute! Maybe I could get lost with them for a day. Tenegrief, Amazon slave! How was your mess and maintenance week, House Mouse?*

"I'm just sayin' I wouldn't blame ya if ya did smoke weed. It's a stupid, closed-minded law written by stupid, closed-minded people. America is supposed to be, at least in principle, mindful of the notion of freedom. I mean, isn't that what marines fight for in the first place—for freedom, freedom of religion, freedom of choice? I mean if an alternative or a competitor of alcohol or aspirin or freakin' orange soda doesn't make you hurt others or retard Americans' pursuit of happiness, then it should be assumed to be produced and consumed on the free market with all the laws and protections of a legitimate enterprise. Shouldn't it be? Am I right?"

"Sir, aye, sir!"

"I just believe if they made it legal, the world wouldn't end. I think teenage use would probably go down or stay the same. Ya know, ya take away the forbidden fruit aspect, and drug use actually goes down, probably. I mean why do we have churches or mosques or synagogues, really? I don't think most Americans would let anything get in the way of their relationship with God. I don't get it. It's like a phobia or something. There must be something I can't see about this. And it's not a gateway drug. Alcohol is the gateway drug. I guarantee that is the first thing anyone does. And that is completely overlooking all the drugs and meds Americans take from the day they are born. What happens when you get sick? Mommy gives you a pill to make you feel better. That's the freakin' gateway.

"People say marijuana takes away your motivation. What does everyone have to be so freakin' motivated about anyways? You smoke a joint and you're content, man. Contentment, man. Contentment is a beautiful thing, man."

Again the two drive in silence for a spell. Two marine F4 fighter jets go streaking across the sky.

"It could raise millions in tax revenues alone," says the strange gunnery sergeant, starting back up his rant. "I mean, sure, there are bad aspects to marijuana; like everything these days, there is a possibility of abuse, sure. But that argument can be used for refined sugar or caffeine. That's how you get all these lard asses everywhere. You need restraint and control in most everything we do as modern people in the twentieth century. You know, most people on the right and the left believe grass should be legalized. It has to be the pharmaceutical companies that are just fleecing the shit out of the American public and their crooked-ass politicians that are in the drug companies' pockets that keep it forbidden.

"Take the Rastafarians, for instance. They believe that marijuana makes them closer to their God, even. Smoking grass is their religion! I mean, come on! I mean, just on constitutional principles alone, for crying out loud! How about freedom of religion? Am I right?"

"Sir, aye, sir."

"Tenegrief! When was prohibition?"

"Sir, the prohibition on alcohol was from 1920 to 1933, sir."

"Haven't we learned anything from that period in American history? If you're not tits in math and science, you should still know your history, at least. And what a history is ours! Oo rah, the Marine Corps!"

"Oo rah!"

"I mean you still couldn't drive while intoxicated. I doubt bosses would appreciate their employees being all stoned out. You couldn't go to work that way. Probably, you still wouldn't be able to smoke on the streets in public—just like alcohol, I suppose. There would still be a huge stigma attached for most Americans. I'm sure the religious folks wouldn't condone it in church. But hell, it would actually give the churchy folk more of a purpose. A lot of those people would still hate the shit out of it and want to repeal the repeal. But if good folks want to get high in their own homes after work, well, that's as old as humanity itself, isn't it?"

"Sir, aye, sir."

"Do you read, Tenegrief?"

"Sir, yes, sir!" shouts Teneriffe.

"I like to read about history. Did you know that the Louis and Clark expedition kept alcohol with them as long as they possibly could while they were on their journey to explore the American continent? And they would do *anything* to keep it with them. They had to carry these giant barrels around rapids on land—what do they call it, portage—because at the end of the day, men like to get a buzz. It makes the danger and the grueling fatigue tolerable. It's the gosh durn pioneer spirit! How about the wooden ships that explored the far reaches of the globe? No doubt those navy ships were storing as much alcohol as they could carry. And America itself was started in order to cultivate and export tobacco. Intoxication is a human necessity especially in a society that values hard work. Am I right, Tenegrief?"

"Sir, aye, sir!"

"Freakin' A right, bubba."

THE PLATOON IS ON ITS weeklong wilderness campaign. Mostly, the platoon marches for countless miles. At times they are required to run with rifles at port arms. Teneriffe's feet have gotten used to the black leather boots, which are not nearly as stiff as before. It seems that as his feet and ankles have gotten tougher, the rigid leather has become more flexible. The platoon has marched all day and most nights on miles of tarmac. They still have time in the mornings to run for PT, with the final PT test to come a week after wilderness week. The wilderness week includes a grenade toss, a mock war, a trip inside the gas chamber, a warrior obstacle course that mainly consists of crawling hundreds of yards in the mud, and pugil-stick fighting, but mostly the platoon marches and marches for miles and miles along the rows and rows of giant green pines that line the tarmac.

On the sixth morning at first muster, the platoon wakes. Each recruit shares a pup tent with another. The platoon lines up in formation in four columns along the asphalt in front of a grove of pines. The whole company is bivouacked along this stretch of woods. The different platoons are separated by a distance of about a hundred yards, and the command post is set back deeper in the woods behind the four platoons.

Drill Instructor Staff Sergeant Carpenter bellows, "Why are you always last, Hay Fly? You're last and you're late, late and last! Wipe that smirk off your face, Hay Fly!" Staff Sergeant Carpenter grabs Hay Fly by the collar with both hands. "You disgust me, Private. You can't even line up straight! You're supposed to be here, and you're way over here! Not here! Here! See, you're right here when you should be over here!" As he berates Private Hay Fly, he jerks him around by the collar, back and forth and side to side, like a rag doll.

Oh hell no! I'm gonna run up on him and punch him in the freakin' head. Do it! Do it! Wait ... use your canteen. Yeah! Oh my gosh! No, wait, that's assaulting a superior officer. Someone needs to smash that Neanderthal a good one! And I'm just the monkey to do it! Do it! Do it! Wait, won't they throw you in the frickin' brig? Holy crap! I'm losing it!

Carpenter's forehead is pressed hard against Hay Fly's forehead, and he's yelling. "You make me sick, Hay Fly! You're a piece of crap! I'd like to just end you now! You freakin' low-life shit bag stupid mother freaker! And your mother would thank me for my troubles, you shit stain!"

Oh hell no! I'm freakin' gonna bash his brains in with my mother flippin' boot! Go now! Now! Now!

Teneriffe's whole body tenses, and his brain is on fire. He is between the thought and the action, a millisecond from charging Staff Sergeant Carpenter regardless of the consequences.

"Okay, now! Hold on there, Carpenter. Hold on there, Drill Instructor. How's everybody doing? Good morning, platoon!"

The sound of Gunnery Sergeant Morehouse taking control of the situation immediately calms Teneriffe and keeps him from making a big mistake. Gunnery Sergeant Morehouse greets the platoon as he approaches from the woods with a scowling Sergeant Roebuck one step behind him and to the right. The gunny's utilities are finely starched and bloused perfectly. He glides up from out of a shuttle van, having slept in a bed in the civilized world and not in the woods in a tent.

"Okay, Carpenter. Chill out, man." The senior drill instructor puts his hand on Carpenter's shoulder. Teneriffe notices that the gunny is wearing a gold wedding band and a green, military-style watch. "Okay, Staff Sergeant Carpenter, the captain's out all over the freakin' place here. Calm down, staff sergeant. Calm down."

"Okay, men, come in here a little closer—not classroom but just close ranks here a little. Okay, fine, men. That's good. Eyes," says Senior Drill Instructor Gunnery Sergeant Morehouse in a whisper with his hands on his hips. "The captain is trying to interview all of you recruits one at a time to ask you a few questions. He is close to getting to us, and I want to let yuns know. Now, before any of you start running your mouth about us or anything else and say something stupid that you're gonna regret for the rest of your lives, just remember that he doesn't really care about your well-being. Your DIs are the only ones that really care about you and your pathetic little problems." The gunny has a big, crooked smile, and his arms are raised to his two assistant drill instructors.

"Yeah, I mean we look after yous like little freakin' babies!" says Sergeant Roebuck.

"So if any of yuns think you're smarter than us and know something we don't and talk to the freakin' man, someday you'll understand just how much me, Drill Instructor Staff Sergeant Carpenter, and Drill Instructor Sergeant Roebuck cared for you and looked out after you, and you're gonna be sorry," warns Gunnery Sergeant Morehouse.

"Well put, Senior Drill Instructor Gunnery Sergeant Morehouse," says Staff Sergeant Carpenter, chin tucked and sounding a bit remorseful.

"We treat you better than your own mommy and daddy!" says Sergeant Roebuck in his deep, froggy drill-instructor voice.

"After we dismiss you from formation, for now, I want you to stick around the bivouac area and eat an MRE for breakfast. Practice on your knowledge or read your green monster. We'll be moving out sometime this morning, so be ready when we yell for formation again. Men, you're all looking good. You're starting to come together. We are right in the mix as far as the company contest is concerned. I know this has been a tough week—well a tough couple of weeks—but wilderness week is almost over; tonight is the last night outside. Then it's just really getting ready for the PT test, the drill competition, final inspection, and then finally freakin' graduation. So basic warrior training is almost over, and if you don't do anything too stupid, you'll probably all make it to the fleet.

"You all have been kickin' ass out here in the wilderness. Guide, I thought you killed second platoon's guide in pugil sticks. I thought you knocked his freakin' head off. Also, First Squad Leader Tenegrief, excellent job for winning the series bull-in-the-ring contest. You'll probably get another commendation for that. All of you are looking good like freakin' marines should. First thing we're gonna do when we get back to the world is make an appointment to go and see the barber and get high … and tights. Oo rah!"

"Oo rah!" shouts the platoon together.

"So yous don't look like retards no more," says Sergeant Roebuck with his lip stitched up to one side.

"Fall out!"

After formation, Teneriffe is reading his green monster and inhaling the knowledge within. He sits on the ground Indian style, the sun shining on his face with his back against a big loblolly pine.

"Ten, you're next to see the captain in the CP," says a skinny recruit, Private Brickell, running up to Teneriffe from a path in the woods. "It's up that trail a spell."

Teneriffe double-times through the woods on the little dirt trail up to the command post. He reaches the command tent that rises from the trail. He then stands in line behind two other recruits from different platoons beside the tent, looking out into a little clearing in the woods where the captain sits facing a seated recruit in an interview. After the line has been drawn down, Teneriffe is told to enter the enclosure.

He stops in front of the captain and says with a sharp salute, "Private Teneriffe reporting as ordered."

"At ease, Teneriffe. Have a seat. What I want to do today, and what I've been doing during this whole week, is interviewing all the recruits to see what kind of shape they're in," says Captain Jones. "Now, I want you to speak freely and relax for a moment. I know this whole experience can be overwhelming, mentally and physically, but it doesn't get any easier here or later in the fleet. In fact, Teneriffe, it gets harder," says the captain sternly. "So how are you holding up, Teneriffe? Is everything okay?"

"Sir, I'm fine, sir!"

"How about your drill instructors? Are they treating you fairly? Have you been abused physically or verbally, or have you seen anyone else being physically or verbally abused?"

Carpenter is a psycho. "More than fair, sir. This recruit thinks that Gunnery Sergeant Morehouse, Staff Sergeant Carpenter, and Sergeant Roebuck are the best teachers he's ever had, sir."

"Really?" says the captain, looking a little puzzled. "They are ... something."

"Sir, aye, sir!"

"I see you're First Squad leader again. I thought you'd been fired."

"Sir, they tried some other guys, Captain, but they crashed and burned. It's not so easy being First Squad leader, sir."

"I see, I see. Throwing everyone's asses out of the bull-in-the-ring contest doesn't hurt though, does it,

Tenegrief? You'll be getting a meritorious mast for that at final inspection."

"Sir, thank you, sir. I'll be looking forward to that."

"That is if you're still with us. We still have to see what the colonel has to say on the matter."

Teneriffe's stomach drops. "Sir, yes, sir."

"You look a little worn thin, Teneriffe. Are you getting enough to eat?"

Teneriffe has lost about twenty-five pounds of fat since coming to Parris Island, but he feels good. He feels healthy, light, and strong.

"Sir, three square meals a day, Captain. Thank you, sir."

"Really? 'Cause you look very drawn out," says the captain with concern.

"Sir, I've never felt better, sir."

"Are you sure? Because, I can put you on double rations, Tenegrief."

"Sir, that won't be necessary. I'm really right as rain, sir."

"Okay, I just don't want your mom thinking we starved you out here."

Oh, man!

"Okay, so keep up the good work, and let me know if there is something I can do for you. Got it, Tenegrief?"

"Sir, yes, sir."

"All right. Then I want you to get on back to your platoon, and good luck with the rest of recruit training. Dismissed."

"Dismissed, aye, sir."

Teneriffe double-times back down the winding trail through the pines and, to his surprise, finds that the platoon—in fact, the whole series—has already formed ranks and marched away. The bivouacked campsite is now deserted. Teneriffe can hear the wind in the green pines for a brief second, and he stands transfixed among the neat rows of olive-drab pup tents that flap in the breeze. Finally, after a few moments of resplendent, sunlit solitude, Teneriffe sees the end of the great green column to his right about six hundred yards away marching down the endless asphalt like a monstrous green serpent.

I do feel a little worn thin. I could be a little drawn out. I wish we could get to march a little, though. That's just what I need. We're not getting enough boot time, for sure.

Teneriffe's eyes begin to well up with tears as he double-times down the tarmac to catch up with the platoons, carrying his rifle at port arms.

"WHAT IS YOUR TENTH GENERAL order?" asks Senior Drill Instructor Gunnery Sergeant Mesceri.

"Sir, this marine's tenth general order is to salute all officers and all colors and standards not cased, sir," replies Teneriffe.

Teneriffe is on fire watch being questioned by the officer of the day, Senior Drill Instructor Gunnery Sergeant Mesceri. The officer of the day can be a drill instructors or one of the battalion or regimental officers, and the officer of the day's purpose includes checking on fire watches to make sure they are walking their posts. This gunnery sergeant is the senior drill instructor for one of the other platoons in the series. His platoon is the most competitive group with Teneriffe's platoon.

"What is your eleventh general order?"

"Sir, this marine's eleventh general order is to be especially watchful at night and during the time for challenging, to challenge all persons on or near my post, and to allow no one to pass without proper authority, sir."

"What are the four lifesaving steps?"

"Sir, the four lifesaving steps are to restore the breathing, stop the bleeding, protect the wound, and treat for shock, sir."

"What is the best way to stop bleeding?"

"Sir, the best way to stop bleeding is to apply direct pressure to a wound using a pressure dressing, sir."

"Is there another way to stop the bleeding?"

"Sir, yes, sir. The other way to stop the bleeding is to use a tourniquet, sir."

"What are two ways to purify drinking water?"

"Sir, two ways to purify drinking water are iodine tablets or boiling the water, sir."

"What does ALICE pack stand for?"

"Sir, ALICE pack stands for all-purpose, light-weight, individual carrying equipment, sir."'

"Describe the M16A2."

"Sir, the M16A2 service rifle is a five-point-five-six millimeter, magazine-fed, gas-operated, air-cooled shoulder weapon, sir."

"What is a stoppage?"

"Sir, a stoppage is an unintentional interruption in the cycle of operation of the service rifle. Some common causes are faulty ammo or a faulty magazine, sir."

"What is immediate action for the M16A2?"

"Sir, immediate action for the M16A2 is to tap up on the bottom of the magazine, to pull back the charging handle, to look for the casing or the cartridge to eject, to release the charging handle, and to strike the forward assist assembly to properly seat the bolt, sir."

"What is battle sight zero?"

"Sir, battle sight zero is a predetermined sight adjustment that, set on a weapon, will enable the shooter to engage targets effectively at ranges when battle conditions do not permit exact sight settings, sir."

"What is the defensive mission of the marine rifle squad?"

"Sir, the defensive mission of the marine rifle squad is to repel the enemy's assault by fire and close combat, sir."

"What are the different colors on military maps, and what do they identify?"

"Sir, the different colors on a military map are red, green, blue, brown, and black, sir. Red lines identify main roads, green is trees and grasslands, blue is bodies of water like lakes or streams, brown is contour lines, and black is manmade features, sir."

"That's not bad, Teneriffe," says Gunnery Sergeant Mesceri. "Not bad at all. I guess you're ready for the test. How 'bout final drill tomorrow? Is your platoon ready?"

"Sir, we're highly motivated to do well, sir."

"Oh, why is that?"

"Sir, Senior Drill Instructor Gunnery Sergeant Morehouse says if we don't win, he's goin' to put his boot far up our asses, sir."

"Ha! Well, good luck then, Teneriffe, and good luck tomorrow. Carry on, fire watch."

"Thank you, sir. Carry on, aye, sir."

Teneriffe watches the gunnery sergeant disappear into the interior ladder well. Private Bulloch, a dark green marine, the other fire watch walking the dark squad bay this night, comes up beside Teneriffe.

"Wow, what was that all about?"

"Ah, just more fun and games."

"Hey, Ten, you nervous 'bout tomorrow?" asks the shy, giant Private Bulloch.

"Nah. How 'bout you?"

"Nah," says Private Bulloch. "What are they gonna do if we mess up—shave our heads and send us to boot camp?" Both the young recruits share a laugh. "Hey, Ten, why do they call this the fire watch? I've been on fire watch a hundred times now, and I ain't seen no fires yet." Then Bulloch gives a deep, jolly belly laugh.

"Ya know, I've been thinking about that for a while, and I think I know why," says Teneriffe. "See, marines have been on navy ships for hundreds of years, even when boats were made of wood. Back then, marines were the captain's bodyguards. Now, the greatest threat to a wooden boat would have to be fires getting out of control and burning the whole ship down, I imagine. But, see, they still had to have fire on board for cooking and smithing and other things, I suppose. So I believe we stay awake to make sure no fires get out of control."

"I was only jokin'," says Bulloch.

"I know, but I heard that one already."

"Oh," says Bulloch. "Well, ya know, it could be that if you were by a campfire late at night, you would assign someone to stay awake so the fire don't go out."

"That's true," says Teneriffe. "I didn't think about that. Or maybe marines stay awake at night to watch to see if an enemy ship opens fire on their ship in order to sound the alarm. Ya know, like to sound the alarm in case of fire or disorder."

"Ya know what I really think it be?" says Bulloch. "I think it's 'cause it sounds so badass … fire watch!" Both the marines again share a laugh.

"Yeah, fire watch. Where you from, Bulloch?"

"I's from Mississippi." Bulloch smiles, showing big white teeth.

"Oh Lord, every light green guy I ever met from Mississippi was racist as hell," says Teneriffe.

"Oh, now that ain't true. That ain't true," says Bulloch. "There's one or two that ain't racist."

"I had this good ol' boy tell me this joke one time," says Teneriffe. "When does a black guy become a nigger?"

"I don't know. When does a black guy become a nigger?" says Private Bulloch, looking a bit menacing. The big white teeth disappear behind thick brown lips.

"When he leaves the room," laughs Teneriffe.

"Oh, see now that's true—that's true," says Bulloch. "Now that sure as hell be the truth."

Then it gets quiet for a while, and Teneriffe worries that maybe he has hurt Private Bulloch's feelings. "Well, ya know, there's a lot less of that shit in the military. Cookie Jarvis says the military has always been ahead of the rest of the country when it comes to race and other social issues."

"Oh, Cookie Jarvis say, Cookie Jarvis say," laughs Private Bulloch. "Yeah, well, I guess a nigger can die jus' as good as one of them white boys for his country," says big Bulloch, not so much joking this time.

TENERIFFE SITS IN A WOODEN chair in the regimental headquarters outside of the colonel's office. A few hours earlier, Teneriffe was in the drill instructors' cramped office, surrounded by all three of his drill instructors, who were speaking freely and fussing over his appearance. They were all checking his uniform and getting him ready for his last appointment on the chain of command for consideration of his positive urinalysis for marijuana.

"Well, this is it, Tenegrief. You're gonna be standing tall in front of the man," said Gunnery Sergeant Morehouse, fixing Teneriffe's collar. "I don't know how you got this far, but whatever you been doin', keep it up. I been in the Marine Corps for sixteen years, and I ain't never had to stand tall in front of the man before."

"Me either, Tenegrief," said Sergeant Roebuck, "but here you are after only three months. You better be strapped in and good to go, Marine."

"Sir, yes, sir!"

"I ain't never been in front of the man neither. I can't decide if this is good for you or incredibly bad," said Staff Sergeant Carpenter while brushing the lint off Teneriffe's shoulders with his giant mitts. "Just for freakin' heaven's sake, don't freak up, and remember everything we freakin' taught you, and you'll do freakin' fine."

"Sir, yes, sir."

Now he sits on the threshold of his last big interview. Teneriffe looks at the floor, which, just like the one in the drug exemption officer's office, is made of shiny wooden planks. He is in the finest shape of his life. He has been initiated into a Spartan training regimen that only a few are given the opportunity to undertake. At least he has that, if nothing else—if indeed the colonel decides to send him home without graduating.

The sergeant major approaches Teneriffe, and Teneriffe stands at attention. The sergeant major is a short spark plug of a man. He is thick. His neck and appendages are bulky and muscular. The sergeant major is also darkly tanned.

"Okay, Teneriffe, you're about to go in and see the colonel. I'm going to go in first, and then I want you to come into the office and report to the colonel. I want you to answer the colonel's questions honesty and sincerely. Don't eyeball the colonel. Remember your bearing, and you should do fine. Got it, Marine?"

"Sir, aye, sir," says Teneriffe.

The sergeant major, who wears three stripes up, four stripes down, and a star in the center of a patch on the upper arm of his shirt, goes into the office and stands beside the colonel's desk. Then Teneriffe passes through the opening. He strides to a few feet in front of the large wooden desk and says, "Sir, Private Teneriffe reporting as ordered, sir."

Teneriffe locks his vision to a point on the wall and never takes his eyes off the spot. His stature is straight and still. He hardly dares to look at the colonel, but he can just make out a gray flattop and tan arms sitting on a big desk. The colonel holds a pen in his right hand and has a brown folder opened across a desk blotter.

"Well, Teneriffe, what do you think of the situation you find yourself in?" says the gray-haired colonel with the silver eagles on his collar.

"Sir, this recruit just wants to be a marine more than ever, sir."

"Does your father know what you've been going through here at basic training?"

"Sir, no, sir."

"What do you think he would say about your situation if he knew?"

"Sir, this private's father would be very disappointed if he knew his situation for sure, sir."

"Well, if you do graduate from Parris Island, you would only be the second recruit to be positive on the drug test since the inception of the drug-screening program to do so. So *if* you do graduate, you need to take this as a wake-up call, Marine. Take this as a second and final chance and stay the hell off drugs! You may have an opportunity to start fresh; please do so, Private Tenegrief! I'm sure you've been told of our zero-tolerance policy out in the fleet. And that is the way it is, and that is the way we like it! Got it?" the colonel says sternly.

"Sir, aye, sir!"

"Now, tell me, Teneriffe, does your mother know what's been going on with you at Parris Island?"

"Sir, no, sir."

"Really?" says the colonel, somewhat bemused.

"Sir, no, sir. I have tried to write and call her often, but I have not worried her with details about my special difficulties, sir."

"Well, I have to tell you, I'm sure she knows something is wrong. Your mom," says the regimental commander, repeating himself, "your mom has called the company office regularly and the battalion twice, and I know for a fact that she reached regiment at least once."

The sergeant major laughs and says, "I wouldn't be surprised if she's been in contact with the commandant of the Marine Corps and the secretary of defense." Both the sergeant major and the colonel laugh some more.

Oh my God!

"All I know, Teneriffe, is you better give that lady a big hug and kiss when you see her again," says the colonel.

"Sir, aye, sir."

"Well, you must have impressed the drug exemption officer, Staff Sergeant Benning, because he seems to think the world of you. And it appears that your drill instructors think you have a little potential to do well for yourself and the Marine Corps. Captain Jones and Gunny Morehouse say you're not a completely lost cause; however, it is still a troubling situation. I really can't say how I feel about you graduating just yet. The sergeant major and I are going to have to discuss this further after you leave."

Teneriffe is a little dejected at not having an answer to his special situation on the spot. He is optimistic, though, partly because the two tough marines were amused enough to be laughing. It was definitely different from most of his other interviews about his failed urinalysis. However, he is guarded and disciplined enough from the many weeks of warrior training not to let any of his emotions appear outwardly in his bearing. Teneriffe remains tall and straight and focused.

Teneriffe skulks in a massive rock cave with weary dread, clothed in rags and dangling chains from his shackled wrists and ankles. The vast rock ceiling is a hundred feet high, and the cavernous underground chamber is lit by only a single fire in a distant corner. The horror of the place is overwhelming. The stench of sweat and urine and smoke hangs all around. Bloody stains and shit streak the walls and dirty floor. Teneriffe can see the mouth of the cave like a gash or a wound in the pale rock edifice. It's above him and to his left. The sky has never looked so beautiful. It is laid out like a dark blue tapestry arrayed with uncountable twinkling stars. Adrenalin surges through his body, carried by the blood coursing through his pounding heart. Something is wrong. The thundering of a heartbeat is all he can hear. Menacing figures begin to approach the center of the crypt. A cold, grotesque realization that he must kill or be killed rips Teneriffe's pounding heart. The approaching assassins are wearing turbans around their heads, and they are armed with scimitars.

Teneriffe growls, "I'm gonna rip off your head and skull fuck you! You Saracen son of a—"

"Ten, wake up!" says Cookie Jarvis, rousing Teneriffe from his rack. "Ten, wake up! They're gonna blanket party Hay Fly!"

"When?" says Teneriffe, jumping out of his rack and rubbing his eyes.

"Right now!" whispers Cookie Jarvis.

Cookie wears his green camouflaged utilities with green war belt wrapped around his potbelly. Cookie is covered, and his star–shaped cap almost appears starched like his trousers and crisply bloused camouflage utility top. His sleeves are rolled up around his dangly upper arms.

Both recruits head to the far end of the squad bay. Teneriffe runs, but Cookie Jarvis jogs, and his gait has sort of a waddle in it. There are about twenty recruits in their skivvies with green shirts tied around their faces converging on the sleeping Private Hay Fly. Each green ninja has a green sock dangling with a bar of soap in the toe.

Hay Fly's rack is a mess. His white sheets and green blanket lie on the concrete floor, having been kicked off in the course of the night. Hay Fly has one arm over his head, and the other arm lies peacefully on his belly. Drool pools from his gaping mouth. One foot sticks out from the rack; a green sock hangs barely on his toes. The other sock is off in the bedclothes and will not be found in time for dressing.

Hay Fly, dude, wake up!

"Look, hold on there," says Teneriffe, stepping into the center of this blanket party and against the right side of Hay Fly's rack. "Wait a second, you guys. What's going on? You all have so much energy you don't need to sleep? They're not training you hard enough?"

"Look, Tenegrief, freak off already. You're not even a squad leader anymore, so why don't you get the freak out of the way?" says one of the masked recruits. Teneriffe was replaced earlier in the day as squad leader, because he was unavailable during the regular training schedule while he was being interviewed by the regimental commander.

"I may not be a squad leader, but I can still give the DIs your names, *Cubano*, like your guide does."

"Oh, he doesn't give them any of our names anymore, *cabrón*."

"Is this about the platoon going to the beach today?"

"As a matter of fact, yes, it is, and Hay Fly is the reason we all got sent there. And you weren't even there, so freak off, Tenegrief," sneers Private Cubano. The masked recruits move in closer toward the sleeping Hay Fly.

"Wait, hold on here a second, this is bullshit," says Teneriffe. "If y'all want to whale on someone, then whale on me. But nobody's gonna freakin' touch Hay Fly!"

"Oh, yes we are, jerk weed, and if you get in the way, we're gonna touch you too, Tenegrief," says Private Royals.

"Look, I was in the captain's office today waiting to go see the colonel, and I saw the platoon's daily training schedule, and it freakin' said exactly what time the platoon was scheduled to go to the freakin' beach. It had us going at fifteen hundred, and it don't have nothin' to do with the Hay Fly. Just because the DIs fuck with Hay Fly doesn't mean we have to. It's all bullshit games. Look, you don't believe me? I'll tell you what we're havin' for lunch tomorrow—ketchup on bread with cheese!" For some reason, thinking about that crappy mess-hall pizza sends Teneriffe into an instant rage, and he is ready to fight. "Oh freak it! Let's go!" Teneriffe assumes a fighting stance.

The masked recruits in the blanket party seem frozen in place. Teneriffe's words have made an impression, but these are highly motivated devil dogs set to forgo some much-needed sleep in order to accomplish their mission.

At this moment, one of the fire watch, Private Bulloch, in camouflaged utilities, green camouflaged cover, and war belt, marches down the squad bay and stands between the blanket party and Teneriffe.

"Let's go, Recruits. Hit the sack. If the duty come by, it be my ass."

Bulloch raises his large, square jaw and tilts his head back, exposing his huge, marble-white teeth spread out into a smile. Bulloch taps the stock of his M16A2.

"Let's go now. Hit the racks, gentlemens."

The members of the blanket party slowly fade back into the darkness and are gone back to their racks. Private Bulloch looks at Teneriffe and smiles and gives him a wink and a nod.

Teneriffe's heart pounds in his chest, and he growls, "Hay Fly ... clap your freakin' mail!"

Teneriffe walks the center of the gloomy squad bay and wearily climbs atop his rack.

Hay Fly lifts his head and says with half-open eyes, "Huh? Wha? Who's there?"

THE PLATOON MARCHES TO FINAL inspection for the graduating series on the main Parris Island parade ground. The platoon is finished with drill competition, and now drill is more fun and less of a worry. The recruits, just a few short days from graduation as United States Marines, really plant their heels in the ground when they march.

The men have been preparing for days now for the final inspection, which is basically an oral exam. The platoon has also cleaned rifles and gone over every detail of their dress uniforms. In fact, the soon-to-be marines will be turning their rifles in to the armory after the inspection, which is itself stressful, because the armorers may refuse to accept a weapon if it is dirty.

The drill instructors sing to the platoon in turns. "Low, righty, lay, oh, low, righty, low."

After a few miles, Gunnery Sergeant Morehouse yells for First Squad Leader Tenegrief to fall back to the rear of the formation. "You're no longer First Squad leader, Tenegrief!"

"Aye, sir!" acknowledges Teneriffe as he double-times to the rear of the formation.

"The *man* has determined that provided that you don't freak up from here on out, you will be allowed to graduate with your platoon, Tenegrief, at graduation ceremony!"

Teneriffe is elated. Although the closer he has come to graduation, the better he has felt about his chances of graduating, he never has been quite sure of the outcome. And although he felt that all his interviews went as well as could be expected—the coincidental bonding with the drug exemption officer and the colonel speaking positively about his future in the fleet marine force—he always has been aware of the twisted Marine Corps sensibility that would delight in snatching him at the last minute from the ranks of the graduating marine recruits and sending him on a bus ride home as a failure. At last, after hearing the gunny's proclamation, an enormous weight has been lifted from his shoulders. Apparently his platoon is happy as well, for Teneriffe receives pats on his back and shoulders and a few smacks to the back of his head.

"That's right, Tenegrief, you're gonna be a real-life marine and graduate with the rest of your platoon!" says Senior Drill Instructor Gunnery Sergeant Morehouse.

The platoon marches on for a little ways.

"But," says the gunny, remembering more of the details, "you won't be getting any of your meritorious masts or any promotion from PI! And if you were a bonus program, chances are you lost that too. Welcome to the suck, Marine!" spits Gunnery Sergeant Morehouse.

"You signed the mother freakin' contract!" barks Sergeant Roebuck.

After a few moments, Gunnery Sergeant Morehouse says agitatedly, "You better wipe that friggin' smile off your face, Tenegrief!"

"Aye, Senior Drill Instructor Gunnery Sergeant Morehouse, sir!" Teneriffe shouts at the top of his lungs.

After marching for a long time to reach the special parade ground in their green dress service uniforms and at rifle arms, the platoon stops beside the other green platoons of the graduating series. The platoons are stacked like cordwood on the edges of the concrete quadrangle.

Gunnery Sergeant Morehouse's arms have three red chevrons up, two down, and crossed rifles in the center. On his forearms are five red service stripes. The drill instructors wear the campaign covers that all soldiers in the United States Army and Marines wore in the late nineteenth and early twentieth centuries. Drill instructors wear these Smokey Bear covers with all their uniforms except when wearing a helmet in full battle gear. The DI's hat sits slanted down toward the nose like a bulldog, and a leather strap secures the cover from around the back of the head. On his chest, the gunnery sergeant's green coat has rows of colorful service ribbons and awards and two shiny medals signifying that the gunnery sergeant is a rifle expert and a pistol expert.

"Platoon, halt! Port arms! Left face! Order arms!" barks Gunnery Sergeant Morehouse. "Parade rest!"

It's nice just not to be marchin' in these dress shoes anymore. A buzz fills Teneriffe's ears. *Ah! My old friends are back.*

Teneriffe suppresses the urge to swat at the sand fleas on his neck and ears.

"Special honor detail, fall back to the rear of the formation and line up!" commands the senior drill instructor.

The guide, who wears a dress blue uniform, and Private Hay Fly go behind the rest of the platoon, which is lined up in four rows.

"Fill in those spots! Cover up, cover up! Tenegrief! Get over here!" yells Gunnery Sergeant Morehouse.

Teneriffe, from the back of the platoon, comes running around to the front of the platoon, which faces the middle of the concrete parade ground.

"Get there, Tenegrief—where the guide was!"

Teneriffe fills the first spot in the front row. Drill Instructor Sergeant Roebuck takes Teneriffe's black M16A2, five-point-five-six millimeter, semiautomatic rifle with parade-slung black hemp rifle strap, and Drill Instructor Staff Sergeant Carpenter hands Teneriffe the shiny wooden guidon stick with a red flag and yellow lettering and the yellow Marine Corps seal. Teneriffe puts the metal silver pike of the guidon stick on the tarmac, quickly extends his right hand, folds his left hand behind his back, and stands fast at parade rest.

Although Gunny Morehouse is an exemplary marine, he does have a defiant, independent streak. His platoon once again did not win the series final drill competition but was judged to have come in second, losing by only a few points. He told his platoon to be proud, for he was proud of them; and he told them all that he thought that the outcome was pure political bullshit and was not based

173

on what actually happened on the drill field. Teneriffe thinks that maybe Gunnery Sergeant Morehouse is stickin' it to the man this time by letting him hold the guidon stick in the front of the formation for the final inspection. Sometimes Teneriffe thinks that Gunnery Sergeant Morehouse really doesn't care what the officers think.

The platoon waits under the scorching sun in their green dress coats and khaki ties for some time. The drill instructors mill about the platoon, looking over the marines and generally joking around. The company's officers and staff do the same, though they seem more interested in the honor details that have formed behind all the platoons. Two platoons have one marine in dress blues, one platoon has none, and one platoon has two marines in dress blues. These marines, including the guide, were secretly measured for their free dress blue uniforms and are to receive a meritorious promotion to private first class, or PFC, and are assured of lance corporal in only a few short months. The patch on the guide's arm is one gold chevron up. Then there are marines dressed in green service suits like the other graduating recruits; however, these marines are receiving meritorious service awards from the silver general and his staff. This is why Private Hay Fly is standing next to the guide—to receive a meritorious mast for his outstanding performance on the rifle range.

After some time, the inspecting officers begin their exam of the graduating series. The platoons wait for a long time as the officers inspect every marine in every platoon. Two or three officers challenge each column of the platoon with knowledge questions and rifle inspection. Just as the officer of the day did with the special guard detail many weeks earlier, the inspecting officers move down the line from right to left, always moving closer to the squad leaders and guide.

After some time, the inspecting officers get closer to Teneriffe's end of the platoon. And at last the inspecting officer, who now appears to be a general, is almost done questioning the private to the left of Teneriffe.

"I do not know the answer at this time, sir, but I will find out as soon as possible on my own or with the help of my drill instructors, sir!" Teneriffe hears Private Gregs say to the general.

"We haven't been pampering you here, have we, Private?" laughs the general. "What are you gonna do out in the fleet where there are no drill instructors, son?"

"Sir, I will follow my chain of command, sir!" shouts Private Gregs.

"Very good, Private Gregs. Good luck and congratulations," says the general.

Sergeant Carpenter steps up and takes the guidon stick from Teneriffe and hands him his weapon back.

Now that's more like it.

The silver general does a right face and squares himself in front of Teneriffe. Teneriffe throws his rifle up to his left hand above his chin and does inspection arms. The silver stars flash in the sun, and the general snatches Teneriffe's rifle from his grasp just as Teneriffe releases it.

Oh, I'm really, really not in favor of that.

"What's your name, Private?" Asks the general, handing Teneriffe back his weapon.

Teneriffe cuts the rifle down to his right side again, with the butt of the rifle on the ground and the flash suppressor and sights in his right hand. His left hand is flat and slanted as in a salute. He cuts his left hand back to his left trouser leg with his thumb along the seam, chest out, chin up. "Sir, Private Teneriffe, sir!"

"Where are you from, Private?"

"Sir, this private is from Warner Robins, Georgia, sir."

"Hoping to see more of the world in the Marine Corps, Private?"

"Sir, yes, sir."

"Did you know marines are assigned to every US embassy throughout the world as security?"

"Sir, I did not know that, sir."

"You would make a good embassy guard, I think, Tenegrief. What's your ninth general order, Marine?"

"Sir, this marine's ninth general order is to call the corporal of the guard in any case not covered by instructions, sir!"

"What is deadly force?"

"Sir, deadly force is the force one uses to cause death or serious bodily injury, sir!"

"When is the use of deadly force justified?"

"Sir, deadly force is justified in circumstances as a last resort when all lesser means have failed or cannot reasonably be employed, sir!"

"What are you, some sort of freakin' know-it-all, Private?"

"Sir, no, sir! This marine just prefers to spend his spare time reading a lot, sir!"

"Oh, that's a good thing, Private. So then, what's your favorite book, Marine?"

"Sir, this marine's favorite book is *The Last Lion,* sir!"

"Oh, that's about Churchill, right? Not bad for a Brit."

"Sir, Churchill's mother was an American, sir!"

"Oh, is that right? Who wrote that?"

"Sir, Sergeant William Manchester wrote *The Last Lion,* sir."

"*Sergeant* William Manchester? He's a marine?"

"Sir, yes, sir. Served in World War II in the island hopping campaign, sir."

"Well, how interesting is that? I'm always telling my wife that marines can be very accomplished at things other than killing. But she doesn't believe me. What about you, Teneriffe? Are you a killer?"

"Sir, aye, sir!"

"Well, very good! But keep up your reading, Private. You might have to fall back on something. The marines will pay for you to take college courses on your way to a college degree. It's one of the many perks to being a United States Marine. So look, Private, good luck in the Marine Corps. Use the service to get what you want, because the Marine Corps is going to get what they want from you. Make sure you take advantage of the GI Bill, and keep it clean, okay, Tenegrief? Got it?"

"Sir, aye, sir!"

Teneriffe stands tall and proud. He has passed final inspection. Dressed in his green suit and tie with his hands on his rifle, he scans the distant horizon. It is a good day to be a marine.

The silver general strides with his green staff closer to the middle of the parade tarmac, and they turn around in formation. All the senior drill instructors are in front of their platoons. A sergeant major standing next to the general yells, "Honor details, post!"

The line of recruits marches out from behind the platoons to about ten yards in front of the senior drill instructors.

"All hear these present greetings ..."

Look at Hay Fly standing tall next to the guide. Oh wow, that guy in dress blues from one of the platoons is being promoted to lance corporal out of basic. Wow! Oh well. I don't think I'll be coming back anytime soon.

It's a few days before Teneriffe ships out to Parris Island and basic training. Teneriffe grabs a stack of pizzas from the pizza warmers and runs toward the glass door. He stops before the entrance and reads the time from the digital clock above. It reads 3:50. He looks at the pizzas stacked in two thermal hot bags and shouts, "Ten, fifteen ... uh ... twenty-three, twenty-five, late, and late ... and crap, two two-liter Cokes. Dang! I'll come back for the Cokes."

Just then another driver, a short, sandy-haired California teenager, comes through the door. "Come on, Rudy, man, stop answering the fuckin' phones, dude!"

"For real, Rudy. Come on, dude," agrees Teneriffe.

Rudy, the manager, stands at the phone banks, where blinking red lights show many lines still on hold. With a phone in each hand pressed to his chest, which is covered with a red apron almost entirely white now from hours of tossing flour and dough, he says, "Well, thanks, you two, for volunteering to close tonight. You dudes are all right in my book." Rudy says this with a big, crooked smile.

The smile vanishes. "Ten, take the free ones last, and both of you, the speed limit on base is twenty-five miles an hour, and if you go twenty-six, the MPs will bust your asses, okay?"

"You know we're closers anyway, man!" the California teen grumbles as he walks to the back with four red pizza-warming bags in each hand and under his arms. Teneriffe runs out the doorway into the yellow, sodium-lit darkness.

Later, in the early-morning gloom, the two Air Force brats lean against their cars. The long hiss of an inhalation pierces the quiet, and the red cherry at the end of a joint glows red.

"Hey, dude, don't be a Bogart."

"Sorry. 'Ere."

"So what did you hear about the Marine Corps?"

"Well, the recruiter says there's no chance of me being accepted, because I failed the eye test. But we submitted some more documents and stuff to try and get a medical waiver. I wrote an essay saying how I've played football, basketball, and baseball my whole life without any problems physically. And I had to say stuff about how much I've always … uh … always wanted to be a marine."

"'Ere. That sucks. You'd've made a kick-ass, heavy-metal, fuckin' hard-rockin', rebel-yellin', Warner Robins Demon marine, dude! Whew!"

"I'm a Northside Eagle."

"Oh, dude, turn this song up … Children of the sun! Children of the sun! Children of the sun!"

The little California pizza dude sings along with the radio. Teneriffe smiles grandly. The light of dawn is beginning to overpower the darkness. There is a brilliant red sky off to the east. And the little dude sings, "Every man, every woman, and every child!"

Later that morning, Teneriffe and his mom are sitting at the antique breakfast table sharing a cup of coffee and talking about the news.

Teneriffe's mom answers the phone. "It's the recruiter!" She hands the phone to him with a worried look on her face.

"Hello."

"I have great news, Teneriffe. Your medical waiver was approved. I can't freakin' believe it," says the recruiter on the other end of the connection. "They're gonna accept your blind ass. You're gonna be a hard-chargin' devil dog!"

"Wow, holy shit! No way! That's totally radical, dude," says Teneriffe. "When? When am I leaving?"

"Well … that's the thing; you have to leave tomorrow."

"Huh? Tomorrow? Get the hell outta here."

"Yeah, you gotta ship out tomorrow. That's the only way we could jury-rig this thing," says the recruiter. "Congratulations! You're gonna be a marine!"

"Tomorrow," says Teneriffe. "But, Sergeant, I ain't really been studying too hard for that piss test. How about giving me another month or something?"

"Oh! What? Nah, we can't do it. You gotta go tomorrow. Anyway, don't worry about it; you're a drug waiver, right?"

"Well … yeah … I guess."

"Okay, then I'll come by tomorrow morning, and you know what to bring, right?"

"No, sir."

"Don't bring shit!"

Ah, Teneriffe!
I'm kneeling—still—

—Emily Dickinson

FOUR MONTHS AFTER BOOT-CAMP GRADUATION, Teneriffe and Private First Class Cubano pass each other after dismissal from artillery school at Fort Sill, Oklahoma. The two marines, along with a few others, muster on the front stoop of the old white-and-green two-story wooden barracks. The marines are all wishing each other well and saying their good-byes before taking leave for home and then final assignment in the fleet marine force.

"Did you call your mother? She's gonna be very mad at you, little cabrón," says Private Cubano, wagging his finger at Teneriffe.

"Very funny," says Teneriffe. "Where did you get, Cubano?"

"I got Camp Lejune. What about you?"

"I got Hawaii," says Teneriffe.

"You lucky dog, you." Cubano smiles broadly.

"I know. Thanks."

Teneriffe again feels very happy with his assignment. Only the top five students in artillery school get to choose their location in the fleet marine force, and Teneriffe is one of them. And those five almost always choose Hawaii. What a change of events. Only a few months ago, Teneriffe was struggling mightily to even make it as a marine, and now his first station is going to be in paradise.

"How 'bout that Cookie Jarvis?" laughs Cubano. "Where is he, anyway? You gonna take him with you?"

"He's around here somewhere. Yeah, he got Hawaii too," says Teneriffe, feeling a bit puzzled.

"Hey, Tenegrief, I wanted to tell you something before we don't see each other no more. The night in boot camp when you stopped us from giving Hay Fly a blanket party was crazy, *loco*. I never seen nothing like it, cabrón. It was something like out of a movie."

This makes Teneriffe smile, and he says, "Well, I'm sorry if I ruined your blanket party, Cubano."

"Oh hell, don't worry about it, Ten; we still had a few blanket parties on the guide."

"What? No way!" says Teneriffe.

"Oh yeah, cabrón. The best thing about it was that you would be sleeping right above it all like a baby. It made us all crack up."

"You're kidding," laughs Teneriffe.

Teneriffe realizes that Cubano isn't joking, and for a moment he becomes sad that he wasn't able to help the guide.

"Yeah, we didn't like the guide; we all thought you should have been the guide, cabrón," says Cubano.

This cheers Teneriffe's mood a little.

"Well, really, with that piss test stuff I was going through, it really wasn't possible … besides, Cubano, I always thought you should have been the guide. Cookie Jarvis too."

Private Cubano seems to grow in height, and his chest is out.

"Wow, really? Ya think so? I would have liked that, cabrón. I think I should have been guide too."

"Sure, well, maybe next time," says Teneriffe. Both men laugh.

"I don't think I'll be going back, Ten," says Cubano.

"I think the next time you go back to Parris Island, it will be as a drill instructor."

"Hey, that would be cool," says Cubano. "You really think so?"

"Definitely. You'd be a kick-ass drill instructor."

"Well, the weather was better there," says Cubano. "I mean it was hot, and the sand fleas were a bitch, cabrón, but this Oklahoma weather is just ridiculous, homes."

"I know, really," says Teneriffe.

"I mean the first two weeks here it was the coldest weather I've ever known, then it rained for a month straight, and now it's the hottest I've ever seen, cabrón," says Cubano.

"I know, and now look at that sunset. Is that the most awesome sight you've ever seen?" All the marines on the cement steps stand proudly and look west at the blazing twilight. *Sunset—reviews her Sapphire Regiment! Day— drops you her Red Adieu!*

Printed in the United States
By Bookmasters